# THE METHODS
# OF SERGEANT
# CLUFF

# THE METHODS OF SERGEANT CLUFF

*Gil North*

*With an Introduction by*
MARTIN EDWARDS

This edition published 2016 by
The British Library
96 Euston Road
London
NW1 2DB

Originally published in 1961 by Chapman & Hall Ltd

Cataloguing in Publication Data

A catalogue record for this book is
available from the British Library

ISBN 978 0 7123 5647 3

Typeset by Tetragon, London
Printed and bound by
TJ International Ltd, Padstow, PL28 8RW

# INTRODUCTION

After battling for justice, at great personal risk, in his first recorded case, Sergeant Caleb Cluff made a swift return to duty in *The Methods of Sergeant Cluff*. The story opens one wet and windy night, with the discovery of a young woman's corpse lying face down on the cobblestones of a passageway in the Yorkshire town of Gunnarshaw. The deceased is Jane Trundle, an attractive girl who worked as an assistant in a chemist's shop. She yearned for the good life, and Cluff finds more money in her handbag than she would have earned in wages.

There are echoes of Sherlock Holmes ("You know my methods, Watson") in the title, and in an exchange in the first chapter between Cluff and Superintendent Patterson, but Cluff is very much his own man. Little that goes on in and around the mean streets of Gunnarshaw escapes him. He is scornful of detectives who rely solely on supposed facts: "More than facts were in question here, the intangible, invisible passions of human beings." Understanding those passions leads him gradually towards the truth about Jane's murder.

In his own distinctive way, the Sergeant shares several characteristics with fiction's more celebrated detectives. He is, for instance, a rather dour loner:

"I'm not married," Cluff said. "I've no children of my own."

"You're lucky. You don't know how lucky you are."

Cluff neither agreed nor disagreed.

He is also a maverick who is the despair of his superior, the hapless Inspector Mole. Superintendent Patterson has more faith in him, but this is frequently tested, as when Cluff insists that one suspect "knows something". When Patterson asks what evidence he has, Cluff simply retorts, "It's true all the same."

Yet he gets results, and is admired because of it, as a conversation between two fellow residents of Gunnarshaw illustrates:

"It doesn't pay to tangle with Cluff."

"You wait," the stall-holder prophesied. "Caleb'll show him."

In the fullness of time, the stall-holder is proved right, although another killing has by then taken place. The mood throughout is downbeat, rather in keeping with the climate of Gunnarshaw—a town modelled on Skipton, "the gateway to the Dales", where Cluff's creator was born and bred.

Gil North was the name under which Geoffrey Horne (1916–1988) wrote a dozen crime novels, eleven of which recorded Cluff's cases. The Cluff series appeared between 1960 and 1972, and a stand-alone called *A Corpse for Kofi Katt* was published in 1978. Horne, who started writing after retiring from the Colonial Service, began by publishing several books under his own name, including a thriller, *The Portuguese Diamonds*, which appeared in 1961. This was shortly before Cluff's popularity led to his unexpectedly hi-jacking his creator's career.

Before long, Cluff made the transition from printed page to small screen. When North was first approached by the BBC with a view to adapting his own work, he was less than enthusiastic, and declined to attend a meeting in London (a place he said he hated). Undeterred, eager television executives travelled to the north of England in the hope of persuading him to write a script. Cluff duly appeared as the protagonist in an episode of the superb television anthology series *Detective*. The programme was introduced by Rupert Davies, the actor who had shot to fame as a result of playing Inspector Maigret, the detective hero of novels by Georges Simenon which were a significant influence on the Cluff books.

"The Drawing" was broadcast on 16 April 1964, with a theme tune composed by John Addison, later well known for his film scores. Leslie Sands played the Sergeant, a perfect piece of casting. Sands, the son of a Bradford mill-worker, had previously written crime thrillers for the stage, and had also acted in and written scripts for *Z Cars*. He made the part his own, and the success of the show promptly led to the commissioning of a spin-off series, *Cluff*.

Leslie Sands took great pains over choosing his props—tweed suit, pipe, chestnut walking stick, together with a specially made tweed hat. The series featured Eric Barker as Inspector Mole as well as a host of equally well-known television actors of the Sixties, such as Glynn Edwards, Rodney Bewes and James Bolam. A second series, this time comprising thirteen episodes, began in the spring of 1965. Michael Bates took over as Mole, and cast members included Leonard Rossiter, Derek Fowlds and Diana Coupland. Leslie Sands' wife Pauline Williams played Mrs Mole in several episodes. In all, twenty fifty-minute stories were broadcast. Although the first series has been lost to posterity, as the result of the BBC's short-sighted policy of wiping tapes, the second series survives in the BBC archives. It has never been made commercially available on DVD.

Each episode was scripted by Gil North. His son Josh recalls that "he liked to be in charge of things", perhaps a legacy of his time as an administrator in Africa, and this was a good way of ensuring that the integrity of his detective's character was not compromised. Intriguingly, each of the television stories was a fresh one; they were not based on the plots of the novels. Yet this industrious author produced thirteen scripts for the second series in the space of a mere six months; ideas about plots came easily to him, he told a local journalist, although he felt that punitive rates of income tax deterred successful writers from being highly productive.

*Cluff* was filmed in and around Skipton, where North had grown up, and where his widow Betty and Josh still live; his daughter Sarah lives in Australia, with her two sons, two daughters, and two grandsons. At its height, *Cluff* regularly attracted twelve million viewers, an extraordinarily high figure by modern standards. One fan who became a cartoonist for the *Northern Echo* in the Nineties adopted the alias "Cluff" as a small tribute to a show that, even then, was largely forgotten.

But the Cluff books deserve to be remembered. Their uncompromisingly laconic style was not to everyone's taste. The distinguished novelist and critic for *The Times*, H.R.F. Keating, had reservations about it. Yet Keating acknowledged that North was "showing us a unique regional voice, and asserting its merits". To this day, his books remain short, snappy, and very readable.

MARTIN EDWARDS
www.martinedwardsbooks.com

# CHAPTER I

T HE CONSTABLE WATCHED HIM SWING ACROSS THE DESERTED
High Street, from the corner by the church. Modern lighting
bathed the macadam in an eerie blue. The front of his Burberry was
dark with wet. Water matted the grouse feather in his sodden, tweed
hat. His thick trousers, heavy with rain, hung shapeless below the
hem of his coat. The tip of his stout stick kept time with the solid
tread of his mud-spattered boots. The big collie at his heels stayed
close, tongue lolling, tense.

The constable stepped out of the shadows.

"Sergeant," the constable said, showing no surprise to see Cluff on
foot. "Round there," he added, pointing. "I think they'd given you up."

Cluff nodded, without stopping. The clock in the church tower
began to chime, four strokes for each quarter, eleven longer ones,
deeper in tone and more widely spaced, for the hour.

He turned off the High Street into a narrow roadway, little more
than a passage, by the side windows of a Victorian Town Hall. The
doors of the public conveniences to his right were closed, the signs
above them unlit. Wind funnelled from the moors, moaning. Rain
dripped disconsolately from crumbling cornices.

A gas-lamp, on a bracket fixed to the wall at the corner beyond
the conveniences, flickered uncertainly. He rounded the corner,
under the lamp, into a cobbled area walled on three sides. The explo-
sion of a flash-bulb made him blink. He halted, the dog's muzzle
cold against the fingers of his free hand. The headlights of a police
car, its engine cut, blazed on men milling restlessly.

Inspector Mole, neatly uniformed, detached himself from a group of lesser officers. The dog retreated, growling. Mole remembered the Sergeant's recent experiences and the Sergeant's present standing with his superiors. The Inspector gritted his teeth, biting back the sarcasm with which he usually greeted Cluff's dog.

Mole mustered a smile. Envious and insincere, he remarked, "We thought you weren't coming, Caleb. It's more than an hour since I rang you." He stifled an exclamation of annoyance at Cluff's lack of excuses. He said, "I couldn't help it. I got on to Patterson at County H.Q. He wanted you to know."

Cluff told him, "We arranged it like that before I went on leave."

The Sergeant stalked forward, past the photographer already dismantling his tripod, policemen moving to let him through.

"What's the use of a single C.I.D. man in a division this size?" Mole asked. "Do they think crimes are going to happen one at a time?"

"You've been busy," Cluff said.

"Someone has to be," Mole answered, unable to suppress his feelings, throwing a glance over his shoulder to ascertain the present whereabouts of the dog. The dog growled again.

Cluff, without looking round, ordered, "Sit, Clive!" Clive sank to his haunches, lips withdrawn from pointed, white teeth, ripples of excitement flowing under the loose skin on his back.

A little, dapper man, brisk, straightened and rubbed his palms together busily. She lay face down on the stones, her arms flung out, her legs splayed, her thighs bared in her fall. Cluff looked at her head. A transparent, plastic hood, tied under her chin, draped her shoulders.

"Well?"

"Isn't it obvious?" the surgeon replied.

A dark patch marred the brightness of her hair, spun-gold in the car lights. Dark threads patterned an ivory nape and lost identity in the rain on the cobbles.

The surgeon demanded irritably, "What's going on in Gunnarshaw? What have they been getting away with all these years?"

Cluff, his belly large, bent with difficulty. He rolled the girl over. Mole, taking a handbag from one of the attendant constables, held it out and said, "We found this." The Sergeant, his eyes fixed on the girl's face, ignored him.

"You don't need me," the surgeon interrupted. "I can't do any more here."

"How long ago?" Cluff said.

"On a night like this!" the surgeon exclaimed. "In this cold! With this rain! I'm not a witch-doctor. Wait for the post-mortem."

"She's—" Mole started to say, opening the handbag.

"I know who she is," Cluff stopped him.

Mole pushed the envelope he was pulling out back into the bag. "Of course," he said bitterly. "I was forgetting. You were born and bred in these parts. You know everybody." He watched the movement of Cluff's eyes. He went on, "There wasn't anything else. I've been over the place with a fine-tooth comb."

"If you're looking for a blunt instrument," the surgeon broke in, a little spitefully, "you've got quite a choice." The surgeon buttoned his raincoat: "You might intend to stay here all night. I don't."

"Clive!" Cluff called. He opened the rear door of the police car and got inside after the dog. A driver came to life amongst the spectators and moved hurriedly for his seat. Cluff, peering out, informed no one in particular, "You can take her away. Let her parents know."

Mole spoke to a constable, taking the envelope from the bag a second time and holding it while the constable copied down the address. The Inspector climbed into the car, ostentatiously choosing his place next to the driver, making it silently clear that he preferred to be as far away from the dog as possible.

At the police-station Constable Barker, on the desk, rose to his feet when they entered. Barker snapped his fingers at Clive. "Good dog," he said. Clive's tail wagged. Clive crossed obediently to Barker and allowed the constable to scratch him on the head.

Barker, young and eager, his cheeks flushed with embarrassment, murmured, "I'm glad to see you, Sergeant. I hope you're feeling better."

"He's in my office," Mole interrupted, opening a door and leading the way.

A youth about eighteen years old, his face dead-white, his limbs trembling, huddled small on an upright chair. Occasionally a more violent twitching afflicted his body. His wide-open eyes stared into infinity and he gulped frequently as if fighting nausea.

Mole settled himself behind a desk. He stabbed a finger in the youth's direction. He explained, "He found her."

Cluff put a hand on the youth's shoulder and the youth cringed. "I'm sorry, Jim," Cluff said. "Can you tell me about it?"

The youth swallowed hard, his lips dry. Cluff wandered to a window. He lifted the blind at one edge and looked at the rain-swept night.

"It's late," Cluff added.

Mole coughed.

"Was Molly with you?" Cluff said.

Jim's words cleared the obstruction of his parched throat. They tumbled over each other: "We weren't supposed to be there. I said we were going to the pictures."

"It'll have to come out now."

"I didn't know what to do," Jim pleaded.

"It was the only thing you could do."

"She's dead, isn't she?" Jim asked, reading his answer in the eloquence of Cluff's broad back. "You'll keep Molly out of it?"

"As much as I can."

"I came out of the lavatory," Jim said. "I was waiting for Molly. Someone ran out of that yard behind."

"A man?"

"It's dark there, Mr. Cluff. That lamp at the corner doesn't give much light. It was raining too. I wasn't taking much notice."

"Think, Jim."

Jim said, "I suppose it must have been a man. I'd have noticed a woman's legs, whiter—"

Cluff turned from the window: "What sort of man?"

"'What sort of man?'" Jim echoed.

Mole picked up a pencil and began to tap on the desk-top. He thought, "What can you expect from them?" disgusted with the people of Gunnarshaw.

"A big man? A little man?"

Jim hesitated: "Not big."

"He saw you?"

The youth considered: "He ran away. By the Town Hall. Into the darkness—"

"Towards the car park?"

"That's why I went—round the corner. At first I couldn't see anything. Then I heard Molly—"

The Sergeant opened the door. He shouted, "Barker!" Barker stopped fondling Clive.

Cluff said, "Get the driver to run Jim home."

They heard the car drive away. Mole put his pencil down: "Was that all?"

Cluff looked at him.

Mole said, "It's up to you, Caleb. There's not much chance for the uniformed branch when you're about." He paused and went on, in a sharper tone, "It shouldn't be difficult, not in a town this size, where everyone knows what there is to know about everybody else." He climbed to his feet: "My wife'll be waiting up. I'd better be moving."

Cluff stayed put. Mole shifted from foot to foot. He forced another cough. He commented loudly, "It's after midnight." The handbag lay on the desk. He offered it to Cluff: "You'll want this."

Mole asked, "You'll take the car when it gets back?"

The Sergeant walked into the outer office, clutching the handbag.

Cluff turned for a second door, leading into his own room. The door closed. Although not in the habit of familiarity with inferiors Mole couldn't prevent himself from informing Barker, "He's no different. You wouldn't accuse him of charging at a job like a bull at a barn-door."

"He gets there just the same," Barker retorted, rousing an anger in Mole that expressed itself in the violent slamming of the door to the street.

Clive stood by Barker's desk. Barker fidgeted, uneasy at the dog's stillness. The ticking of the clock on the wall filled the room.

The sashes in the windows rattled. Flurries of rain attacked the window panes.

Barker went suddenly to the frosted glass panel behind which Cluff had disappeared. He tapped with his knuckles. He found the knob and twisted it.

Cluff slumped in a chair, on the other side of a table, his hat tipped over his closed eyes, fists thrust into the pockets of his Burberry, trouser legs steaming slightly under the table. Clive, sedate, walked forward and settled himself on the floor. Barker tiptoed away, easing the door to, missing the flicker of Cluff's eyelids.

The police car returned. Its driver stamped into the outer office, a gesture from Barker pleading for silence. "Is he going home?" the driver asked.

"Who?"

The driver glanced at Cluff's door.

"Hasn't he got his car?"

"Not him!"

"He's asleep."

The driver said, "It's not the night or the time I'd have chosen for a stroll. You could have knocked me down with a feather when he finally turned up with that dog of his. He wouldn't get away with it anywhere except in Gunnarshaw."

"Let him rest."

"She wasn't half a bobby-dazzler," the driver commented.

Alone in the office Barker crossed from time to time to Cluff's door, pausing to listen. He could hear nothing except the ticking of the clock and the wind and the rain. Gunnarshaw slept, its streets empty, the only lamps still lit those at road junctions, the rows of terrace houses climbing the slopes of the moors dark and quiet. Barker found it hard to believe that anyone else was alive in the town. He was a little afraid in case Cluff should be unable to repeat the one important success that stood to his name, solicitous for Cluff, disturbed. Cluff's heavy, jowled face persisted in his mind, lined, the hint of greying hair peeping from under Cluff's hat. He looked older to Barker in repose, more careworn, less competent.

Barker jumped, startled by the discordant ringing of the telephone. A woman's voice, pitched in too loud a tone, demanded peremptorily, "Is he there?"

"I'll put you through."

He switched over to Cluff's extension, prepared for a slight delay before Cluff woke. The Sergeant answered at once. Barker said, "It's Mrs. Croft."

"I'm not in."

"I've already told her—" Barker began and Cluff's phone banged on the rest.

Barker went back to the outside line and excused himself lamely, "I can't get hold of him."

"Very likely!"

"A woman's been killed."

"Again!"

"They sent for him last night."

"He's the only policeman in Gunnarshaw?"

"It's a job for the C.I.D."

"He's got Clive with him?"

"Yes."

"That's something. Who are you?"

"Barker."

"The young one? I want him here by eight."

"I don't know—"

The telephone said, "He's not fit to be let loose on his own," and died.

"She wants you back, Sergeant," Barker said, avoiding Cluff's red-rimmed eyes, Cluff's grey dewlaps covered with a stubble of grey whisker.

"Is it still raining?"

Barker shook his head.

"Get me Patterson. At his house."

Cluff's phone said, "Caleb?"

"It's me."

"I expected a call."

"Did you?"

The Superintendent at County Police Headquarters said, "Sooner or later."

The seconds ticked away.

"Where are you?" Patterson asked.

"The station."

"A pity it's come just now."

"My God!" Cluff said. "What else do you think I had to do with Wright dead and Jinny Cricklethwaite in prison?"

"I told Mole—"

"Whose job is it?"

"I'll send you an extra man—"

"What for?"

"You can't handle this alone."

"He'll do more harm than good in a place like Gunnarshaw."

"Where have you got to?"

"I haven't started yet."

The telephone stayed quiet.

"Don't you trust me?" Cluff said.

"You have your methods."

"Leave it then."

"It isn't me. The Chief Constable—"

"All right. Someone local."

"We haven't—"

"There's a man in the uniformed branch here. Barker."

"I'll arrange it with his Superintendent. Mole won't like it."

"Never mind Mole."

"Can we help in the laboratories?"

"I'll let you know. It was raining last night. Mole searched for a weapon. He didn't find one."

"Put something on paper and let me have it," Patterson was saying when Cluff rang off.

The Sergeant rubbed his eyes. Clive stretched. The dog approached Cluff and put his head on Cluff's thigh. Cluff looked at his watch. "In a while, boy," he said.

He reached for the handbag Mole had turned over to him. He fingered apart the metal claws fastening it and up-ended the bag, allowing its contents to drip on to the dirty sheet of blotting-paper that served him, when he wrote, for a writing-pad. The articles came slowly, obstructed by the letter that had revealed the girl's identity to Mole. They piled in a little heap, a lipstick, a packet of cigarettes, a box of matches, a powder compact, loose coins. The letter arched at the mouth of the bag, blocking an object too bulky to slip past its edges.

He removed the letter and a folded wallet joined the other debris of her life. The Sergeant dealt with the wallet first, counting out twenty-five pounds in one-pound notes, crisp, straight from a bank.

He took the letter from its envelope and read it. It told him nothing that he hadn't known, or guessed in the course of the night. What he knew or suspected others in the town must know or suspect equally.

His face set obstinately. He sat staring at the currency notes. At first they worried him but, after a time, he saw them differently. He began to be glad of the notes.

# CHAPTER II

T HE FINGERS OF THE ROUND CLOCK ON THE OFFICE WALL
crept to the hour. Cluff's door remained stubbornly shut. The
chimes of the clock in the church tower sounded across the roofs.

Barker handed over his duty.

The telephone in the outer office rang. Cluff appeared abruptly,
stuffing letter and wallet into the bottom of a pocket, Clive bound-
ing in front of him. He marched smartly to the main door and into
the street, calling to Barker. Behind them they left the man on the
desk open-mouthed, gaping at the receiver, stunned by the flow
of Annie Croft's invective.

The town, squat in its narrow valley, brooded, shrinking into
itself under the threat of the leaning moors, only half awake in the
winter dawn. A boy on a motor-scooter, a bag of newspapers slung
from one shoulder, chugged by on his morning delivery. A man in
overalls, grease-spotted and oil-stained, rode past on a squeaking
bicycle, lifting a hand to Cluff on the pavement. Milk-bottles rattled
in one of the side-streets. A harsher note from the High Street a
few hundred yards away betrayed the arrival of the first buses from
villages scattered sparse in the neighbouring dales.

The cold morning, damp from the night's rain, the keen edge to
the wind driving through a gap in the hills that encircled the town,
the grim expressions, characteristic of Gunnarshaw, on the faces of
the people he saw, brought Cluff back nearer to his normal frame
of mind. In the daylight, at least, he knew where he was, everything
about him solid and familiar. He flexed his muscles, allowing his big

body to go slack and then grow taut again. A vague ache that had pervaded his limbs since his experiences in the blazing barn at Ghyll End lessened. He sniffed the morning, conscious of the first pangs of appetite. A stone lay on the edge of the kerb. Cluff aimed at it with the tip of his stick and sent it leapfrogging into the carriageway.

"Don't you lodge over there?" Cluff asked Barker. "Go and change," the Sergeant added. "Have breakfast with me."

He went back into the police-station while Barker was away and told the man on the desk, "Send the car for me about ten. The driver can wait at the bottom of the lane. I'll come down."

He walked along the pavement, allowing Clive to range in front, the dog like the man in a brighter mood. When Barker, in civilian clothes, overtook them Cluff said, "We'll walk. What's the country for?"

A man with a handcart, sweeping the gutter, jerked his head at Cluff and the Sergeant jerked his head in return, an exchange of greetings more economical than words but just as effective.

An entry separated a row of houses from a line of shops extending on to the centre of the town. He turned into it with Barker and they emerged into the forecourt of a garage belonging to a road haulier. They walked to iron-barred gates in a wall and through the gates, going left, leaving a car-park in their rear, passing the side of the Town Hall.

Cluff stopped at the cobbled area behind the public conveniences. The cobbles were wet, blades of grass pushing between them. A cat, scratching to cover its dirt in a corner, flew past them, spitting. Crudely-drawn faces in chalk, the work of children, grinned from the paintless, nailed-shut doors of what had once been the stables of a coaching-inn. A young hand had scrawled in ill-formed capitals, "Jack loves Mary," and added as an afterthought, "Jack is daft," underlining the verb heavily.

"You wouldn't know," Cluff said.

A caretaker materialized in the doorway of the men's half of the conveniences. He remarked, "By gum, Caleb, this is a fine how-d'ye-do. They won't be standing courting round here for a bit."

"It's no good asking if you saw anything?"

"You know as well as me how they come and canoodle round the back. I don't watch them. I'm past that."

Cluff started to move on.

"You'll not have to look far," the caretaker assured him. "They may have cheek but they've no gumption. You wouldn't think they were Gunnarshaw bred, most of them."

Barker put out a hand, too late, to pull Cluff back as he stepped off the pavement. Cluff continued on his way serenely, glancing neither up nor down the High Street, blind to the traffic. The driver of a car trod violently on his brake and stuck his head out of the side-window, ready with an insult. He recognized Cluff and came fully awake, catching Barker's eye and winking.

Cluff halted again on the opposite pavement, examining this side of the street, his gaze wandering past the entrance to a public library, its grille still in position, beyond a bank and a service station and shops with their blinds drawn.

"It's too early," Barker said.

Cluff hesitated, like a man who didn't know his own mind.

Barker offered, "I'll wait."

"They've nowhere to run to," Cluff replied. "Not in Gunnarshaw."

The shops and offices gave way to rows of cottages, old, each row marked by a date carved in stone. The town meandered, unplanned. Surprisingly, a farmyard opened off the pavement, with a couple of geese in it and a turkey that gobbled angrily, ruffling its plumage. More houses ended at the top of a long hill and the road levelled for a while, a country road without sidewalks.

In spite of his bulk Cluff moved easily, his pace even. He walked with a long stride, using his stick as a third leg, and Barker grew warm keeping up with him. Muddy ditches, rain-filled, cut furrows in the grass verges. Bare hedges fenced rough pastures mounting to the moors. The moors were dark in colour, the heather dying off. Plantations of fir trees nudged the bases of sheer rock outcrops serrating the skyline. The wind whistled. Sheep in the pastures lifted their heads, wary of the two men and the dog, not trusting in the protection of the hedges. Cluff's cheeks glowed redder, his eyes washed clean of sleep.

A lane, aiming for the moor-top, avenued for a while by ranks of horse-chestnuts, winter-nude, its surface rough, branched from the minor road. It swung, as if the climb had proved too much, and sought an easier trace along the flank of the moor. Cluff, pushing open a white-painted gate, went up a flagged path through a wind-blown garden to the porch of a stone cottage, stone-slated, four-square and low. White hens grubbed outside an old hut in a field over the garden wall. A bull-nosed Morris stood forlornly outside a shed. Cluff said, "I couldn't get it to go last night," more in admiration of the car's independence than in anger.

Smoke curled from a chimney, escaping from the open triangles of flat stones reared edgewise against each other. Mullioned windows, high under the eaves and small to match the gales, leaded into diamond-shaped panes, guarded a massive, nail-studded door. The door opened before they reached it to reveal Annie Croft, as red-cheeked as Cluff, hair blowing in wisps, arms akimbo, as broad as she was long.

"I'm not surprised," Annie said, "you didn't dare face me alone."

"We're hungry," Cluff told her.

"I'm tired of drumming it into you," Annie went on. "You'd be better off with your brother on the farm at Cluff's Head. You're no chicken."

Clive wriggled past her, making along the passage for his bowl in the kitchen. She let them in and Cluff took Barker into the low-ceilinged living-room, where a round, oak table was laid for breakfast. Barker's nostrils twitched at the smell of frying bacon and his mouth watered.

The room was warm, dim in the grey morning, a huge fire blazing in the grate, adding its comfort to the comfort of big chintz-covered armchairs and a couch, to the softness of a thick-piled carpet and the cheerful glint of horse-brasses on the walls. Rough hewn, black-oak beams reached for Barker. An immense cat, long-furred, coiled in a chair on the right of the hearth.

Barker watched the cat, aware of Cluff's movements in the room above, the boards resting on the beams creaking as Cluff crossed backwards and forwards. He could hear Clive eating in the kitchen. The cat's unwinking stare fixed him balefully. Annie busied herself at the table, setting a second place.

"It suits him," Barker said.

"Wonders never cease," Annie remarked. "He's not one for company."

"It's quiet."

"We're used to it."

"I'm not a countryman."

Annie said flatly, "He needs looking after. I only come in in the morning."

"He never married?"

"It's none of your business."

The cat jumped down on to the rug. It stretched delicately and moved towards Barker, appraising him more closely. He put out his hand and the cat backed. Cluff, shaved, but still in the same heavy tweeds, came in from the passage. He sat down in the chair the cat had vacated and the cat, disgusted to have lost its cushion, leapt on to his lap. "Her name's Jenet," Cluff said.

The lids over Barker's eyes drooped. He could hardly believe that they had breakfasted. Cluff, the cat still on his knees, sat in the same position across from Barker, one hand resting lightly on the cat's fur.

Barker relaxed, the room warmer, vaguer, drowsier. If Annie was still in the cottage he couldn't hear her. Clive lay between his chair and the Sergeant's, jaw propped on the fender, gazing open-eyed into the fire, dreaming.

The wind howled a little, intensifying the quiet and the peace. Gunnarshaw, Cluff's duties, his own, seemed a long way off. Somewhere at the back of Barker's mind, deep-down, a realization stirred, a memory of death.

His eyes closed finally and did not open again. He breathed gently, sliding in his seat. His lips parted and his head lolled against the chair back. He slept.

Cluff let him sleep. An hour went by. The Sergeant lifted Jenet and got up. He lowered her into the chair and she was no more awake than Barker. Clive, moving silently, followed the Sergeant.

He reached up to the pegs in the wall of the passage for his hat and coat. He sighed. In the brief space of his gesture he lost track of his intention. He found himself in his garden, shivering after the heat in the living-room. The drab garden, the drab fields, the drab moors, did not offend him. He wasn't a man for summer days, for the brilliance and the long evenings of summer, the small ration of summer dark.

Feet tramped in the lane. The sneck on the garden gate clicked. Cluff said, "I told you to wait in the road."

"I've been waiting," the driver replied. He held out a folded note: "The Inspector sent this. It's urgent."

"To the Inspector everything's urgent."

The driver caught sight of Cluff's old motor-car. "Don't tell me it's broken down again," the driver said.

Annie caught him with his hand on the gate. She shoved his tweed hat and his Burberry at him. "Have you gone crazy," she asked, "or is it high summer?"

He crammed his hat on to his balding head and struggled into his coat. Annie tossed her head towards the cottage: "What about him?"

"Let him sleep."

"I thought it was too good to be true."

"He was up all night."

"Did you sleep in your bed?"

Cluff shook his head at Clive. The dog flattened, his belly close to the ground, his tail sagging.

"I don't care where you're going," Annie said. "You're taking that dog with you. I feel easier when you have it by."

"Mole doesn't like dogs."

"You're your own master. That dog goes with you."

# CHAPTER III

M OLE EYED CLIVE. HE SAID, "YOU'VE BROUGHT YOUR ASSIS-
tant."

"I've had to borrow Barker," Cluff told him. "It wasn't my
doing."

Mole returned, shortly, "They're in there."

"It wasn't necessary."

"I thought I was giving you a hand. It seems to be expected."

"I'd have gone to see them."

"They're not crippled."

"It's hard enough for them as it is."

"They brought her up. She was their daughter."

Cluff opened the door of the interview room. He switched on
the light under its white, porcelain shade, dispelling something of
the gloom. He put his hat and stick on the bare table and threw a
word at Clive.

He studied them, side by side on the old, horse-hair couch set
across the corner. The man especially had an air of unbelief about
him, as if he refused to believe in the situation in which he was
involved. If Cluff hadn't known it he could have told at once they
weren't Gunnarshaw born, nor from anywhere near Gunnarshaw.
The woman was toil-worn, grey-haired. The man had large, red
hands scarred with healed cuts and a thin, furrowed face. They
wore decent clothes, but cheap ones. The cold in the room made
them cold. The man tried to efface himself as much as he could.
He didn't know Cluff except by sight and he was nervous, in the

manner of his class, when confronted by the police. His eyes swam with tears. His wife's face hardened into a grim, forbidding mask.

The silence between them lengthened. Cluff slouched in the upright chair behind the table.

"She was a good girl," the man asserted suddenly, his words too quick, too hopeful, lacking the ring of truth. The silence was more intense afterwards for his outburst. His wife darted at him a rapid look of reproach. He lowered his eyes.

"I trusted her," the man said, striving to convince not Cluff, but himself.

The woman put a hand to her mouth. She had a handkerchief squeezed into a ball in her palm. She pressed the ball of the handkerchief against her pale lips, stifling a protest.

"She was a good girl," Trundle repeated, a note of hysteria in his voice.

Cluff asked, "Her friends?"

"So young," the father murmured. "It seems only like yesterday—"

"It couldn't have been hard," Cluff said, not knowing whether he was telling the truth. "She didn't suffer."

The man sobbed. He had his hands to his eyes, shutting out a picture he hadn't seen but could see only too clearly. His wife stiffened, irritated by his breakdown.

They sat without speaking, awkwardly, able even to hear the ticking of the clock in the outer office. The woman shuffled on the couch, her skirt rasping. Cluff felt her eagerness.

The Sergeant got to his feet abruptly. He pushed his chair back and the legs of the chair scraped harshly on the wooden boards of the floor. The woman's eyes, reflecting the bleakness of her existence, had no softness or pity in them. He read in her face her half-conscious desire to be revenged for the hurts she had endured, the hopes deferred until she was past hoping. The hate she had for her husband mounted in her, the sense of her loss the less because she knew how much more his loss had been.

"I'll get them to take you home," Cluff said.

He opened the door and showed them out. He listened to her whispers on the steps of the police-station, sibilant, unanswered, while they waited for the car to come round. He heard Mole's voice: "What did you get out of them?"

Cluff's lips pressed firmly together.

Mole said, "The woman knows."

"You saw the daughter. Was the mother ever like that?"

"You're right," Mole agreed thoughtfully. "It's hard to believe they're related."

Cluff said, "They had to live together. They couldn't get away from each other. The mother could never get away. The daughter with a chance still left in her life, the mother with none. She'll never forgive her husband. She'd never have forgiven her daughter if her daughter had lived."

"You're lucky. You'll get the facts from her."

"More than the facts."

"The mother didn't kill her." Mole stared at the Sergeant. "Come," he added. "You don't believe that!" He waited. "Well? Why don't you say something?"

"What is there to say?"

Cluff whistled Clive into his office. He sat in his chair, his eyes on the papers with which his table was littered, the pile of files high on his left. He made no effort to transfer them one by one, considered and dealt with, into the empty dip to his right. Now and then he looked at his watch. Clive, as much at home here as in the cottage, dozed.

Mole could not settle. He kept going from his own room into the outer office, stealing surreptitious glances at Cluff's door. "He's not still in there?" he asked the man on the desk and went out before the constable could reply. "Haven't you been in?" he said sometimes. "What's he doing?"

The Inspector's curiosity got the better of him. He poked his head round Cluff's door. He said, "It doesn't matter about Barker," and offered, "I can lend you more men if they'd be of any use." He regarded the confusion on Cluff's table, Cluff's pen dry on its stand, Cluff's pencils blunted and broken. He remarked, "You'll have a job to catch up with that lot."

Cluff put his hat on his head and Clive jumped to his feet.

"Can I give you a lift?" Mole wanted to know.

Cluff left the station.

Mole smouldered, unable to concentrate on his work. He went out to his smart little car, parked tidily round the back, dismally certain that Cluff would turn up results for which he didn't deserve the credit, that the more far-fetched and irrelevant Cluff's ideas were the more likely they would be to approach the truth. The Inspector told himself that, Cluff being Cluff, the murderer would probably walk in by himself and confess.

Mole drove up the High Street on his way home for a meal. The street had wide pavements with trees planted at intervals along the kerbs. Broad ribbons of stone setts ran on both sides between pavements and carriageway. Temporary stalls, selling fruit and fish, drapery and sweets, stood on the setts. An ironmonger had appropriated the space opposite his frontage for a display of gas-cylinders and buckets, rolls of wire and tools. In two or three places collections of farm implements were on show.

The street was busy, the day a market day, the pavements filled with people, only a trickle of them moving, many of them stout men talking in groups, unmistakably from the dales' farms about Gunnarshaw. The whole town seemed to Mole to be populated with Cluffs. He was bedevilled with Cluffs, all dressed as the prototype dressed, with dogs the spit of Cluff's dog, carrying sticks identical with Cluff's stick. Their faces were as round and as heavy and as red. They looked just as solid and as slow.

He caught sight of the real Cluff and braked suddenly to avoid running down a man with a crook. He continued on his way more slowly, but irritable because amongst all these Cluffs he still could not mistake the Cluff who mattered.

Cluff, on the pavement edge by the library, nodded to his doubles, returning their "Calebs" with a "Fred" or a "John" or a "William" or a "Joe". They knew as well as he did what had happened in the town the night before and, to make quite sure, a placard outside a newsagent's broadcast the news to everyone except the blind or the illiterate. He occupied his present position, or one adjacent to it, on every market day and usually they stopped and chatted with him, about their farms and stock, the weather, the prospects for the coming season, accepting him as one of themselves, speaking of Cluff's Head as if it belonged to him as much as to his brother. Today he got only brief acknowledgments. They left him alone apart from their greetings, not presuming on friendship.

A girl came out of a chemist's shop, seventeen or thereabouts, fair-haired, shapely, very fresh and pretty. She paused on the pavement to look up and down the street. She saw Cluff at once and her face turned scarlet. He read panic in her manner. She stood rooted to the spot, staring at her feet as if she hoped the flags would open and swallow her up.

He walked to her. "I remember you," he said and her flush spread down her neck to the collar of her coat. She glanced wildly about and he thought for a moment she was going to take to her heels. He went on quickly, "I saw you watching me from your window in Balaclava Street."

"I didn't know," she told him, in a small voice.

"She worked with you," Cluff said.

"She was older than me."

He waited but she didn't add anything. He asked, "Isn't your name Jean?"

She had her eyes on Clive. "I've always wanted a dog," she said.

"He won't bite."

"Or a cat."

"My brother gets more than he knows what to do with."

The girl uttered a sharp exclamation. Cluff turned to a man who had come up beside him, very neat and clean, in a subdued, unobtrusively checked suit, well pressed and almost new. The man said, "I've been expecting to see you all morning." He had an air of arrogance about him, the appearance of a man who wouldn't take kindly to contradiction. An ostentatious self-importance made up more than adequately for what he lacked in inches. He shot a look of displeasure at Jean, a David to Cluff's Goliath.

Cluff looked down his nose, making no effort to conceal his dislike of little, brash, assertive men.

"I couldn't close the shop," the man said. "I've a duty to the public."

"Trade must have been good this morning."

The Sergeant prodded with his stick at a crack between the flagstones, out of sympathy with men who talked too much, with too much authority, not entirely at his ease, preferring silent men as big as he was. They were alien to each other, Cluff and the chemist. The chemist had a dark-haired, foreign look about him, an urban sparkle, a Celtic restlessness the antithesis of Cluff's northern ancestry, his descent from remote Viking ancestors, close on the sea to the elemental, as close on the holdings they carved out for themselves in the wild country when they drove inland from the coast.

The chemist's shop behind them had a bow window on either side of its recessed entrance, pseudo-antique, reconstructed from the original building to its proprietor's own specifications. The name over the door, gold-lettered, discreet, read "Greensleeve." The shop struck Cluff as pretentious and artificial, a confection in sugar unsuited to the masculine stomachs of a people bred to hardiness. He considered the huge bottles, filled with red and green and blue liquids, on the high shelves at the backs of the window spaces too gay and colourful. He could not remember when ornament and decoration had been valued in Gunnarshaw, when the feminine and tawdry had been accounted higher than the utilitarian.

"You haven't much time," Greensleeve told the girl, "if you're going to be back by one."

Cluff went on poking at the crack between the flags, conscious that the High Street was quieter, interest heightening. He had an impression of pricked ears, of a reduction in the pace of the passers-by, of necks craning and eyes peeping out of the corners of their sockets. Evidently Greensleeve felt it too, stranded with

the Sergeant on a little island of isolation about which the tide of
market day ebbed and flowed.

"We can't talk here," the chemist said.

Cluff followed Greensleeve into the shop. A counter ran down
each side with another transversely between their ends, separated
from them by gaps through which the assistants could pass. In
the wall behind the rear counter an open door gave a glimpse of
a dispensary.

A girl in a white overall, in her late twenties, had the shop to
herself, a long, slender girl with a pinched, sulky expression and
a mouth pulled down at the corners by discontent. She watched
Greensleeve's jaunty progress to the dispensary and her eyes glit-
tered. Cluff nodded to her, receiving in return a look whose meaning he could not interpret.

They sat one on either side of a desk, the door into the shop
closed, the walls about them fitted with shelves. A work-bench, with
a sink at one end, ran under the shelves. A blue flame hissed gently
from a nozzle on a water-heater. Measuring jars and test-tubes,
pestles and mortars, a pill-rolling machine, flasks and other impedi-
menta of a chemist's trade littered the bench. The smell of drugs
was noticeable and not unpleasant, astringent, clean, antiseptic.

A half-smile played on the chemist's lips. Through a window
over Greensleeve's shoulder Cluff could see a yard, walled, with a
big, brown-painted, two-leaved gate of solid planks.

"I've very little help to give you," the chemist interrupted Cluff's
thoughts.

He tried to think back, to the many times before when he had
met Greensleeve in the streets, or seen him in his shop, comparing that Greensleeve with this one, sensing some subtle change.

The Greensleeve condescending to him was a brighter, healthier man than the man he could immediately remember, even more alert, cheerful, in a high good humour. The killing of one of his assistants hadn't touched him. Greensleeve said, as if in answer to Cluff's unspoken question, "After all, Sergeant, she only worked here. Her private life was her own concern."

"True."

A car in the yard, recently washed, still shone with a moist sheen. The brown leaves of the gate stood slightly ajar, revealing a narrow alley joining a road some distance off. Water patched the sloping concrete round the car. It still trickled in a turgid, shallow stream through the open gate, losing itself finally amongst setts like those in the High Street.

"She was only a girl," Cluff said.

A woman crossed the space he could see between the leaves of the gate, from a tumbledown cobbler's shop on one corner to the dingy, blacked-out window of a rag-merchant's on the other.

"Attractive," Cluff added.

A hosepipe sucked at a tap in the yard wall to the right. It snaked, rubbery and supple, for the car, its mouth empty and gaping.

"Possibly," Greensleeve went so far as to agree.

"You must have noticed it."

"I'm older than you are."

"It makes a difference?"

"I've the advantage of you, Sergeant. I've been married for thirty years."

"Of course."

The yard was Greensleeve's, the car Greensleeve's, Greensleeve a power in the town, amongst the most prominent of its citizens, prosperous, respected, a finger in every pie. Cluff's old, stained coat, his battered hat, the uncreased pipes of his trousers contrasted with Greensleeve's smartness, a bull in the presence of a gadfly.

"There's not much for a girl to do in Gunnarshaw," Cluff said.

"Gunnarshaw's the same as a hundred other towns. It has its amusements, harmless maybe, but sufficient—"

"For a girl like that?"

"You assume too much."

A shade of violence in Greensleeve's reply startled him a little. He lifted his head and looked across the desk at the chemist. Greensleeve's fingers busied themselves in shuffling precisely a heap of correspondence. The chemist allowed his sleeve to rumple on his arm so that a gold wristlet-watch appeared.

"I'm keeping you?" Cluff asked.

"It's your privilege."

"That's why she was killed."

"I'm not sure I follow—"

"Because she was young. And pretty."

"If you say so."

"What other reason could there be?"

"You've more facts at your disposal than I have."

Cluff wanted to turn his head to see what it was behind him Greensleeve was staring at. The papers on Greensleeve's desk rustled. Pharmacopoeia and catalogues were stacked on top of a green, brass-bound safe in a corner.

Greensleeve, more uncertainly, told Cluff, "I see you know about him."

The Sergeant waited.

"It's not pleasant for me," Greensleeve excused himself.

"Nor for me."

"He pestered her. I suppose you heard about him from Jean?"

Cluff neither admitted nor denied the chemist's assumption.

"But it can't be," Greensleeve went on. "She'd have nothing to do with him."

Cluff's eyes were vague and empty.

"They couldn't have had anything in common," the chemist persisted.

"A youth?" Cluff said. "Gaunt, with an undernourished look about him? The sleeves of his jacket too short? His trousers climbing up his calves? Boots, not shoes? A flat cap with a broken neb instead of a hat?"

"He couldn't have expected to remain anonymous. The whole town must have seen him at one time or another. He hung about the shop evening after evening."

"Last night as well?"

"Surely you don't need my confirmation?"

"Your word carries weight."

"Every night recently."

"She left with him?"

Greensleeve frowned.

"He followed—?"

"I shouldn't like to feel myself the cause—"

"It's your public duty."

"Put like that—" Greensleeve spread his hands in a gesture of resignation.

"And the time?"

"What time do we all close in Gunnarshaw?"

"I shouldn't have asked."

Cluff moved for the door to the shop. He opened the door. He paused in the doorway, his fingers still clutching the knob, an impression in his mind of rapid, flurried movement. The assistant he had passed on the way in stood behind one of the counters, idly busy with a display of cartons. She breathed quickly, struggling to control her breathing. He stared hard at her. Either she did not realize that the dispensary door had opened or she was pretending not to know he was there.

"You've been helpful," Cluff said over his shoulder, remaining in the doorway.

"I'm glad," Greensleeve said.

"She worked late sometimes."

Greensleeve's voice sounded annoyed. "Occasionally she stayed on to assist me with my returns."

"Not last night?"

"No."

He heard Greensleeve behind him and stepped into the shop. The girl at the counter listened, not watching now what her hands were doing, looking past Cluff at her employer. A carton slipped to the floor. She bent to retrieve it.

Greensleeve ordered, "Go and get your dinner, Margaret."

Cluff walked between the counters, into the street. Clive, sitting on the pavement outside the shop, got up and joined him.

# CHAPTER IV

ATARPAULIN SPREAD AS A WINDBREAK ACROSS THE END OF one of the stalls on the setts hid him from the chemist's.

The High Street was busier, the farmers attending the market joined at this time of day by men and women either on their way to their midday meal or returning from it. Some of them, when they passed where Cluff was standing, either lowered their voices or stopped talking altogether. Others, on the contrary, spoke more loudly. He heard his own name mentioned, and Greensleeve's. They were shop assistants and office workers, a step or so below Greensleeve in the social scale of Gunnarshaw. They didn't like Greensleeve any more than he did, though they could connect Greensleeve as little with the death of Jane Trundle. It was something to them, at least, that she had worked for the chemist, a proof that he wasn't always as removed as he thought from the commoner mass of his fellows. The Sergeant sympathized with them. His prejudices were as strong as theirs. He didn't believe, any more than the people going by, in selfless service, in the labour of love men like Greensleeve quoted in excuse of their political and urban activities.

The course he had to take nagged at him. He knew what he had to do and he had no clear idea of when he was going to do it, or whether he was going to do it at all. He was two men, the Sergeant of Police and Cluff. He feared that what the Sergeant might discover would prove mistaken the innocence in which Cluff believed, with nothing to support belief except Cluff's identity with Gunnarshaw. The unreasoning emotions of Cluff warred with the detachment the

Sergeant was obliged to maintain, the impersonality of the Sergeant
with Cluff's understanding and compassion for people like himself.

Clive recognized a friend amongst the crowd in the street, the
dog's tail wagging, the dog, alert, moving away from Cluff. The
Sergeant and Cluff, rejoined, came back to reality at the touch of
a hand on Sergeant Cluff's shoulder.

Constable Barker said, "Why didn't you wake me up?"

Cluff's car confronted him, parked on the setts between the
stalls.

Barker explained, "I brought it in. In case you needed it. It was
only a blocked feed pipe."

Cluff said, "That sort of thing's a mystery to me."

Greensleeve crossed the pavement from the door of his shop.
Cluff stepped a little out of concealment. He watched Greensleeve
over the road towards a café, a superior type of establishment,
patronized at lunchtime by the more prosperous tradesmen, the
managers of banks, insurance inspectors, chartered accountants,
solicitors, whose tables were permanently reserved. They took more
than a professional interest in the life of Gunnarshaw, sitting on
committees, attending the church as wardens and sidesmen, being
active in charitable causes, some of them, like Greensleeve, serving
on the town council. When the Sergeant ate at all in Gunnarshaw
he chose a humbler place.

"He doesn't live all that far off," Cluff remarked. "It wouldn't
hurt him to go home to eat."

The people in the street expected action from him. Barker, impatient, begged silently for instructions. Cluff's fingers curled round
the letter in his pocket. If he had more facts collected, confirming
the facts he had already, what would he do with them?

"The surgeon—?" Barker suggested.

"We know she's dead."

The letter was definite. The young man waiting outside the shop at night for Jane Trundle was definite. Cluff couldn't gainsay the facts. The facts were clear. He didn't believe in facts, not when interpretation of the facts involved men and women he'd grown up with.

Facts didn't lie to Mole. Cluff closed his eyes to shut out the facts. He wanted to throw away what he knew already and begin again. She hadn't been killed for money, for any material gain. More than facts was in question here, the intangible, invisible passions of human beings. Facts could have one meaning to Mole, another to Barker, still another to Cluff. It wasn't facts that mattered, but what lay behind the facts.

He'd no weapons in his armoury but his own feelings. He wasn't permitted these intuitions, these sentiments that might be false, guiding him not nearer, but farther from the goal he was expected to reach. He admitted the danger of his prejudices, the possibility of cardinal error inherent in his likes and dislikes. A man had to be true to himself.

"The report," Barker was saying. "He must have finished the post-mortem by now."

Cluff said aloud, "No weapon."

Greensleeve, as short as a woman, disappeared into the café.

"And little blood," the Sergeant said.

"The rain washed it away."

Cluff had more in his pocket than the letter, a wallet well filled, fat with notes.

Barker considered, his brow wrinkling. "No," he said. "No. She was killed where you found her."

"Did I say she wasn't?"

Barker argued with himself, unconscious of Cluff's attention: "No one would have carried her through the streets, even on such a night."

"Not in his right mind."

"Who doesn't have a car these days?" Barker added.

"—The people who lived where she lived—"

"Besides," Barker went on. "That boy—Jim—the one who reported it. He saw someone running off."

"I hadn't forgotten."

"It couldn't—"

"What?"

"No one would do a thing like that. Find her, I mean, and then leave her for someone else to find, afraid to get mixed up in it, of questions, inquiries, the police—"

"I shouldn't like to think so."

"But it's possible."

"Anything's possible. It's as well it's me you're talking to and not Mole."

Barker looked embarrassed. He started, "I was—" and stopped. Cluff didn't help him. Barker asked desperately, "Isn't that what you were thinking?"

Barker said nothing for a while. Cluff stayed still. Barker opened his mouth: "You'd seen her too. Her clothes weren't cheap."

"We all knew her in Gunnarshaw."

"What was she doing there? On foot. In the rain. Walking the streets."

"Would we be standing here—?"

"It's not like her. How much did she earn?"

"Six, seven pounds a week at the most."

"She couldn't afford it."

"Was she poor?"

"Her father—"

"I've seen him."

"Then how—?"

"She's dead," Cluff said, a second time since Barker had met him. "She's dead." He smiled at Barker: "Go and see the surgeon then."

He watched Barker's back down the street. The owner of the stall stopped fumbling with a pyramid of oranges. He sidled closer to Cluff. He offered, "I'll keep an eye open, Sergeant, if you like. Are you looking for anyone special?"

"You tell me."

"I wouldn't like to be in your shoes," the man said. "She asked for it."

"You'd see her often."

"Wasn't she worth looking at?" The man paused. "She made the most of it."

"She'd nothing else."

Cluff left him. The stall-holder's wife, returning from a kiosk higher up the street with a steaming mug of tea in one hand and two meat pies on a plate in the other, looked at the Sergeant and then at her husband, lifting her eyebrows in mute question.

The stall-holder said, "He's got on to that young chap who used to hang about the shop."

"He couldn't miss, could he?"

"I'm sorry for the lad. He didn't look to me as if he'd hurt a fly."

"What do you think Caleb Cluff is?"

"I just told him, I wouldn't have his job for all the tea in China."

Cluff stopped by the chemist's. He went in, unaware of the confusion he caused Jean, back now and by herself in the shop. She looked past him, into the street, across the road to the café where Greensleeve was, a tiny spark of fear in her eyes. He toyed with a show-card on the counter.

He asked, "Is it pleasant for you, working here?"

He asked again, "You all left together last night?"

She shook her head: "Jane went early."

"I see."

"She did sometimes."

"I've met her in the streets."

"She wasn't always in the shop. She worked with Mr. Greensleeve as well."

"In the dispensary?"

"He uses it for an office too."

"When the shop's open?"

"She was helping him yesterday afternoon."

Cluff's attention wandered. He didn't seem to be listening.

Jean said, "Ought I to be telling you this? He's my employer."

"Does it matter?"

Jean decided to admit, "She came out of the dispensary in her hat and coat. It couldn't have been more than half past five."

"What did she say to you?"

"Nothing."

"To Margaret?"

"Not to either of us."

"And Mr. Greensleeve?"

"I'm not sure. He came out behind her and followed her to the door."

"It was early for the young man to be waiting."

"You know about him?"

"Does it make it easier for you?"

"He was always there. From soon after five, every evening."

"There wasn't anything regular about her movements."

"I've seen him there—when I've been out—at all times of the night."

"He went after her?"

Jean stared at him: "But they went away together." She said quickly, "It was the first time. She used to walk past him as if he wasn't there."

"Yes?"

"I don't want to get him into trouble."

"Nor do I."

"She went straight up to him. She linked her arm in his. I could see her past Mr. Greensleeve in the doorway. She turned round and looked back at us. It's hard to explain—"

"On purpose?"

"Perhaps—"

The minute finger of an electric clock, with letters spelling out the name of a proprietary medicine instead of figures on its face, jerked hypnotically, fascinating Jean.

"He won't be back yet," Cluff said and Jean knew that he was referring to Greensleeve.

"Margaret will."

"Have you anything else to tell me, Jean?"

"She's coming now."

"I'll go this way," Cluff said, making for the door to the dispensary, Clive behind him. He heard the parting of her lips, the expulsion of her breath, and walked on without looking round.

He closed the door of the dispensary and leaned against it. He had his stick in one hand, the other in the pocket of his Burberry, gripping the letter and Jane Trundle's wallet. His eyes wandered about the room, coming to rest on Greensleeve's desk. He listened to a vague murmur of feminine voices, the accents of question and answer.

Clive waited quietly. He was glad, as he always was, of Clive's presence, easier in Clive's company than in the company of people, of people like Mole and Greensleeve. He divined in the dislike, barely suppressed, that Mole had for him a reflection of the hostility he felt for Greensleeve. The voices in the shop were louder. He could distinguish between them though he could not hear the words. Jean's voice had in it a note of panic. He remembered that if the assistants had the use of a cloakroom it must be through here somewhere.

He went to the desk. He stood looking down at the papers on it. He stared at the drawers on either side of the desk. The safe in the corner attracted his attention and he knew it would be locked.

He was unwilling to leave. He didn't care very much whether Margaret came in and found him, or not. He cared nothing for Greensleeve in spite of Greensleeve's power and position in the town. Something disturbed him and he didn't know what it was. The girl he had seen dead on the cobbles last night had been in this room at this time yesterday. Was it the memory of her living that troubled him, or his own lethargy, his lack of direction, his reluctance to commit himself to a course of action? The day wasted, as he had wasted the night in his office, himself complicating what should be obvious, Greensleeve's writing materials reminding him of the report for Patterson he had not so much as begun. Why was he haunting the chemist's shop? What good was he doing, either to himself or to the law of the land?

The voices continued, complaining, querulous, argumentative. He sensed again an uneasiness in his surroundings, something in the atmosphere on which he couldn't put his finger, which couldn't be real or real only because it was born of his own imaginings. It wasn't enough to allow his contempt for men like Greensleeve to run away with him. If Greensleeve was involved it was only by proximity, by the casual coincidence of his position as Jane's employer. The shop was Greensleeve's, pregnant with the character and the presence of Greensleeve, the material by long association taking on an affinity with the immaterial aura of Greensleeve. Could Jane Trundle too not have left something of herself behind in a place where she had spent so many of her days?

The dead didn't talk; the dead left no part of themselves as memorial. Cluff's visit had no priority, no more conscious intention than his long inaction in the High Street. He had simpler, more direct pointers to his duty. He idled away the hours, chasing chimeras, trying to impress on what was the stamp of what he wanted it to be. Had he hoped to learn anything from Jean? What had Jean to do with it, any more than Greensleeve, any more than Margaret with her bitter mouth, her hard eyes, her life gone sour?

A rear door in the dispensary let him into a short, narrow passage. He postponed leaving by a door on the left of the passage giving on to the yard until he had opened, in turn, two doors on his right. He discovered only a store and a cloakroom.

A few drops of water still glistened on Greensleeve's car, scattered here and there over its smooth bodywork. The broad trail left by water sluicing from the car as the hose was turned on it had almost dried, marking a cleaner track on the concrete, its edges sharply defined. Cleaner, but not quite clean, swilled in consequence of the swilling of the car, the result fortuitous.

Clive rumbled in his throat. The Sergeant retreated into the shallow recess in which the yard door was framed. He heard movement in the dispensary, Margaret on her way to the cloakroom. He abandoned pretence gratefully, accepting the fact of discovery, allowing events to proceed as they would. He stepped into the yard as a leaf of the solid gate creaked and swung farther inwards.

The man wasn't Greensleeve, nor had Cluff expected him to be Greensleeve. He had a leather and dusters in his hands. He went to the car and stood looking at it, not yet aware of Cluff.

Cluff remarked casually, "I didn't know you worked for Greensleeve."

The man whirled, recognizing Cluff's voice, startled, his face taking on an expression of guilt, delving into the depths of his mind to bring up crimes of which Cluff could accuse him. The Sergeant eyed him, grimly amused, eyes a little narrowed, looking as though he knew all the secrets of Gunnarshaw.

"You're off your beat," the man returned, wary, unable to discover in himself a misdemeanour worthy of Cluff's attention. "This is private property."

"You're not usually so fond of work."

"An odd job now and again when we're slack." Tattered clothes, too large for him, hung on his wiry body. Ingrained dirt lined the crevices of his skin on face and neck. A greasy cap covered greasy hair. He wore a handkerchief twisted round his throat. Cracks threaded the uppers of his unpolished, down-at-heel shoes.

"So long as they know at the rag-shop," Cluff said.

"They know where to find me if I'm wanted."

"Don't let me stop you."

The man wiped his leather perfunctorily over the car bonnet, without exerting himself. He dabbed with a duster, resentful of Cluff's supervision. He asked, "Have you nowt better to do?"

"I'm easy," Cluff said. "It does me good to see you working."

The man spat. A murky scrawl appeared on the car.

"They'd make a better job of it at the garage," Cluff remarked.

"They'd be paid more."

"Whatever he gives you, it'll be as much as it's worth."

The leather squealed. The man said, "What are you snooping about for?"

"It doesn't look a job you're used to."

"Is he back?"

"What's your hurry? He won't want it till closing time."

"He was sharp enough this morning about getting it done."

"He must know you like I do."

"You should have seen it when I started."

"The weather's dirty at this time of year."

The man worked for a few moments: "Look here, Mr. Cluff—"

"I'm not after you this time."

"That's a change," the man retorted. "Not that I've done anything."

"If you haven't, you will."

"We get blamed for everything, me and a few others."

"There was a murder in Gunnarshaw last night."

"Here! I'd nowt to do with that."

Tiny black spots of debris, stranded on the concrete as the water had drained away, dotted the yard at Cluff's feet. Lines running diagonally hatched the yard into a pattern of diamond shapes.

Cluff went through the gate, the rag-merchant's warehouse on one side of him, a pile of rubble on the other, where a couple of cottages had been condemned and demolished. The building beyond the site of the cottages, at the corner where the back entrance to Greensleeve's shop joined one of Gunnarshaw's older streets, looked as though it had been lucky to escape destruction. A grimy window stared across at the rag-merchant's. The door Cluff made for was down some steps, the floor on to which he trod below the level of the setts leading from the chemist's yard.

Dust shrouded a small, littered room. A buffing-wheel droned, whirring softly. Cluff leaned on a ramshackle counter, decorated with half-a-dozen rusty tins of shoe polish and a box of laces that might well have been there since the place was built.

The wheel stopped. The cobbler in the space behind the counter swivelled on his stool, feet scraping on discarded scraps of leather, putting a boot down on his bench. Crippled, he limped across to Cluff. One shoulder rose higher than the other and he had the makings of a hump on his back. His eyes, through steel-rimmed glasses bound with twine, were shrewd.

"I thought you'd be in, Caleb."

"You knew more than I did."

"You don't miss much."

"In Gunnarshaw!"

"What's it say in the poem—'time to stand and stare'?"

"I'm not seeing a lot today."

"It'll come when you've mulled it over."

"It's taking its time."

The cobbler rooted in the junk under the counter. He came up with an enamel bowl and held it under a tap near his bench, rinsing it. He hobbled back with it, full, and put it on the floor, calling to Clive. Clive went through a space in the counter, bridged by a hinged flap. The dog put his muzzle into the bowl and lapped noisily.

The cobbler lifted the flap, inviting Cluff into his sanctum.

Cluff perched on an up-ended box. The cobbler returned to his stool. His foot worked a treadle and he held the edge of a sole to his wheel. Clive lay down by Cluff. Cluff hunched forward, slackly, letting his mind go blank.

The cobbler held the boot up at eye-level, turning it in his hands, examining it. He said, "I work late."

Minutes passed before Cluff replied, "You have to with the prices you charge."

"It won't last."

"When's this place coming down?"

"Soon."

"I knew you'd lost at the Inquiry."

"I'd no chance. Not me against the council."

"It'll improve his property when your shop's cleared away."

"He knows that. He's not on the council for nothing."

"You've been here a long time."

"I'm not supposed to know what's good for me."

"None of us are these days."

"Which way did you come?" the cobbler asked.

"Through Greensleeve's yard."

"I'm surprised he let you."

"He wasn't in. He didn't know."

"He'll find out."

"Let him."

"He's a nasty sort to get across with."

"I can look after myself."

"There's too many like him running things."

"In my father's day they had to be gentry. Any Tom, Dick, or Harry with the cheek can stick his oar in now."

"You could retire yourself, Caleb."

"It stops me from thinking. What would I do?"

"There's Cluff's Head."

"John's settled. I'm too old to start farming on my own."

The cobbler set his wheel going again. He worked quietly for a while, finishing the second boot of the pair he was occupied with.

"I've seen her with him in his car," the cobbler said.

"Maybe."

"Late on."

"Coming away from the shop?"

"Aye."

"She helped him with his books."

"He's got a front door."

"It won't wash."

"What makes them tick?" the cobbler demanded.

"He's too much to risk letting it go. His public life's meat and drink to him."

"He rides rough-shod. They get to think they're above the rules."

"I'm paid to be a policeman."

"You know his wife."

"I haven't seen her lately."

"Nobody has."

"Well?"

"She was never much to look at," the cobbler said. "He married her for her money."

"It's not the first time that's happened."

"He's in his fifties."

"I'm not much younger."

"You know what I mean then."

At the door Cluff turned, one foot in the hollow of a worn stone step. He said, "It's not enough, Tom. You can't make bricks without straw."

"You can have a good try."

"It wouldn't get me anywhere."

"They're saying in the town it was young Carter."

Cluff's fingers crumpled the letter in his pocket: "Already?"

The cobbler said, "You don't believe that, Caleb?"

"I shall, if I have to believe it."

# CHAPTER V

C LIVE TROTTED AT HIS HEELS.

He kept away from the centre of the town and away from the police-station. Turning a corner he ran into a uniformed constable. The constable said, "Sergeant, Barker's looking for you. I saw him a while back."

Cluff grunted at the constable and walked on. The constable pushed his helmet sideways on his head and scratched his scalp. But he knew Cluff. He shrugged his shoulders and grinned to himself.

The Sergeant wandered the back streets of Gunnarshaw with no sense of urgency, killing time. He passed the railway station near the outskirts of the town. A high fence of sleepers, placed on end one against another, separated the road along which he was walking with Clive from shunting yards and railway tracks. The afternoon had turned greyer than the morning, and cold. The beginnings of rain spattered him and the wind blew the rain away.

He kept to the pavement on the side of the road opposite to the fence. Gates in garden walls dropped behind him in orderly succession, the gardens they protected scarcely worth the name, mere strips of withered grass, bordered by meagre empty flowerbeds. Soot and ash blackened both grass and soil. The stonework of the terraces fronted by the gardens was grimy, their windows dingy. No one went in or out of the garden gates. The houses themselves betrayed no signs of occupancy.

The pavement shone black ahead of him. The road at his side gleamed black with a film of moisture. The grey of the whole world beyond the road and the pavement took on a deeper hue, adjusting itself to the norm.

At intervals a car, or more infrequently a bus, drove between the terraces and the railway lines. Engines whistled mournfully. The buffers of goods-wagons crashed against each other, kissing violently.

Streets sliced the terraces every few hundred yards, running away from the road, jammed between road and railway on the one hand and the high embankment of a canal on the other.

The Sergeant turned into Charles Street and, halfway along, into Rupert Street, a backwater in a region of backwaters, running parallel to the railway and the terraces by the railway. The back windows in Rupert Street looked at the back windows of the terraces in the distance, divided from them by the long line of yards behind the houses in Charles Street and those of the street next adjoining. The windows of the living-rooms in the middle of Rupert Street had a view, over their own yards, of washing strung on sagging ropes, the permanent greyness of babies' nappies, of children's rompers, and of coalsheds and outdoor lavatories. The houses at either end of the street faced, no less depressingly, the blank gables of the rows going down to the main road.

Cluff ambled in Rupert Street, between the houses on its one side and the many-windowed wall of a high mill on the other. At the other end of the street a jumble of unpainted hen-huts and rusty, wire fences enclosing vegetable gardens spiked with the rotting remains of Brussels sprouts filled an area of open ground, long since denuded of grass. A mangy goat, staked to a tangled rope, looked ownerless and starving.

He leaned against the mill wall, opposite number twelve. The wall vibrated slightly, trembling at the power of the machines racing inside. The grey winter afternoon shaded quickly to the early winter night, daylight dispelled more rapidly by the storeyed building towering at Cluff's back. Pilot-lights in the three lamp-posts on the pavement in front of the houses, one at either end of the street and one halfway along it, sparkled into visibility. Tiny clicks heralded the release of gas to the mantles and the lamps bloomed, wan.

He retraced his steps, into Charles Street, still alone except for the dog, down Charles Street almost to its junction with the road, the front rooms hemming him in as coldly dark and silent as those across from which he had been standing for so long. Unseen, he stopped again in the shadows, glancing now and then over his shoulder towards the mill, aware that it was getting late, afraid of being swamped, before his purpose was accomplished, by the evening flood of the mill's operatives.

He watched the road, where the white pole of a bus-stop reared by the fence of railway sleepers. Cars and lorries drove by, headlights blazing, tyres swishing on the damp macadam. A grey mist began to collect, eddying.

A dark-red, double-decked bus drew up by the stop, ejecting a slim trickle of passengers, the last of them lagging, keeping to himself, a youth, nondescript, unremarkable. He crossed to Charles Street, the sort of youth to be expected in this part of Gunnarshaw, ignorant of the town's real tradition of sheep and farming, recent, the upshot of the mills that had trespassed into the valley with the Industrial Revolution, finding in the climate of the valley and the ample water of the valley the conditions suited to them. Thin and stunted, his boyhood impetus to the exploration of the country about the town long spent, the youth came gangling and loose-limbed, stoop-shouldered, hollow-chested, in a ready-made suit too small for him. A flat cap accentuated the sharpness of his features.

Cluff motioned Clive to stillness. He shrank farther back, hugging the wall of a house. The youth walked like a man in a dream, his eyes cast down, paying no attention to his surroundings. Cluff put out a hand. He let it fall heavily on the youth's shoulder. The youth gasped. His knees gave way and he stumbled. Cluff held him, feeling his bones sharp under his cheap clothes.

"Jack," Cluff said. "Jack Carter."

He saw the youth's face, in the yellow gas-light. The face crumpled, losing shape, white before, whiter now. The youth's bloodless lips worked soundlessly. He shook in Cluff's grip.

"It's all right," Cluff murmured, and kept his hand where it was, cloth bunching in his fingers.

Carter's eyes roved. His head oscillated this way and that on his scrawny neck with its prominent, mobile Adam's apple, jerking like a ball on an elastic string. He shrank from Cluff, an animal at bay, searching uselessly for a way of escape, the pack at its throat. He said, "Don't take me home, Mr. Cluff."

"I've been waiting to see you, Jack," Cluff answered him. "Better here than where you work."

He shepherded Carter down Charles Street, his hold transferred to the youth's arm, and along Rupert Street. In Rupert Street Carter hesitated. He moaned and Cluff had to force him on. He steered Carter into the lee of the mill and round its far end. A siren shrieked in the dark, without warning, making Carter start violently, quivering. Behind them weavers poured from the mill into Charles Street. Cluff said, "Just in time. You wouldn't want them to see you with me."

A narrow path, no wider than one man at a time could pass, crawled between the gable end of the mill and the broken wire fencing the derelict hen-pens and vegetable gardens. The mill cut them off from the illumination of the lamps in Rupert Street. Points of light glimmered distantly, far away on the other side of the waste ground, which lay black and threatening, an ocean of dark. Somewhere a dog barked and Clive snarled in answer. Clinker scraped and splintered on the path. A jet of steam hissed, white, from the bent arm of an outlet pipe over the engine-house of the mill.

In the beam of Cluff's torch a low wall held back the base of the embankment. A gap showed in the wall, its stones pulled down by children, making a way where there was no way. The mill wall ended, its extension up the bank a high railing shutting off the heaps of a coal dump. A long scar in the grass stretched up by the railing to the towpath.

Stones slid and rattled as Carter climbed over them. Carter and Cluff, bent double on the greasy, trodden earth, pulled themselves along, clinging to the bars of the railing. Carter breathed heavily. Cluff kept close to him.

The weeds on the canal bank stirred. Something plopped into the black water, raising a dull splash. Clive, his fur on end, stood forelegs apart on the edge of the bank, nose twitching, head down.

"It's as good a place as any," Cluff said. "We'll not be seen here. Not at this time of day."

Carter drooped.

"You know what they're saying," Cluff added.

"That," Carter replied. "And you."

"I know your father. And your mother."

"They warned me not to have anything to do with her."

"You're old enough to stand on your own feet."

Bare branches of trees across the canal rubbed against each other in the wind. The wind ruffled the water. The water lapped gently at the land.

"I wanted to marry her," Carter burst out.

"Why not? You've known her all your life. You were children together. You've grown up with each other."

The noises of Gunnarshaw floated to them on the wind, muted and unreal. They were closer in their isolation to the dead than to the living.

"I can't believe it," Carter said suddenly. "I can't! I don't know how I've lived through today."

Long minutes dragged endlessly. Cluff's shoulders hunched. He had his hands deep in his pockets, his stick hanging by its handle on one wrist. He loomed big and black and shapeless, a rock, solid, resistant.

"It's not the end of the world," Cluff murmured at last.

"It ended a long time ago."

The minutes lengthened again.

"Jack," Cluff said. After a while he stated, tonelessly, "You were with her last night."

Carter wasn't listening. He wasn't on the canal bank, with the wind blowing chill about him, the houses of Gunnarshaw down there at his back, the house he lived in, the house she lived in. He said, not to Cluff but to himself, "She won't have anything to do with me." He used the present tense not the past, enduring as he

had endured, himself alive and she still alive, continuing his tor-
ment. He couldn't believe either that the child he had played with
had grown into the girl she had become. He couldn't believe it and
he had to believe it.

"I'll have to know," Cluff said.

The youth turned, wondering where he was and who was with
him, coming back slowly to a realization of Cluff, of the inevitability
of Cluff, the impossibility of ever being free from Cluff.

"Get it over with," the youth pleaded. "I can't stand any more
of it."

"I'll believe you, Jack."

"What's the use?"

"Tell me!"

"I was with her. Is there anything you don't know?"

"Everything, Jack," Cluff said. "Everything."

The Sergeant stepped closer to the edge of the bank, blocking
Carter from the water. Carter's eyes stared through the Sergeant
at the canal, large, unblinking. Carter stayed very still. A sob broke
from him. Cluff smelt the air damp and scented with pollution.
Weeds choked the canal. Its banks crumbled. Gases stirred in the
ooze on its bottom, bursting in tiny bubbles on its surface. The
canal was filled with corruption.

Cluff extended his arms, as a barrier or in a gesture of embrace.
He felt rather than saw Carter's hands go to his face, trying to
shut out the scenes his eyes looked on. He heard the groan Carter
uttered. Carter whirled. He jumped for the embankment, slither-
ing, keeping his balance by a miracle, not caring whether he lost
it or what hurt his body took. Carter's arms flailed, useless wings
lacking pinions for flight. He hurtled into the wall at the foot of the

embankment, dislodging stones, the stones crashing and rolling. Cinders on the path crackled under his running feet.

Cluff allowed his own arms to fall to his sides. He let Carter go. He stayed where he was, his heart aching, the night growing quieter for the earthquake of Carter's departure. Clive looked from Cluff to the spot where Carter had vanished and back at the Sergeant, confused, uncertain of what should happen next.

Nothing happened. Cluff continued to stand where Carter had left him. His body shivered with cold. He did not notice the cold. He tried to recall his own youth and it would not come back to him, but he was sorry for youth because youth had to bear so much.

The towpath unrolled, a black ribbon side by side with the ribbon of the water only slightly less black. Cluff followed the ribbon, carrying as burden a sense of defeat. He got past the mill, to the gap that was the end of Charles Street. He listened for the tread of feet in the dark, for the opening of a door and its closing, for voices raised. Clive danced on the path, the dog's every movement urging the man to go on.

He slid awkwardly down the embankment, foothold difficult. The toes of his shoes felt for cracks between the stones of the wall. He walked past the big doors of the mill, blank and lowering, along the upper part of Charles Street to where Rupert Street joined it.

He stopped in Rupert Street, on the pavement outside the door of number twelve. These houses had no bells. He lifted a hand to the knocker, jerking the knocker up and down. Drawn blinds blacked out the window by the door and the two windows on the top storey above his head.

He knocked again, harder. He knew the time it took for a caller at the front to be answered in Rupert Street, the raised brows of the people in their rooms at the back, the certain knowledge that anyone seeking that way of admittance must be making a visit of importance, the minutes necessary to set the rooms to right, to tidy the person.

Feet shuffled in the house. A chain rattled. A key grated in a lock rusty from disuse. The mother, Mrs. Trundle, outlined in a rectangle of light shining into the passage at its farther end, faced him in the doorway. She led him without question along the passage. Steep stairs mounted halfway along, making the passage narrower.

The living-room had a smell compounded of cooking and the body odours of the woman and of her husband, of their daughter too perhaps. The light showed her grey hair, home-tended, muzzed as if she had been sitting with her head in her hands, running her fingers backwards and forwards over her skull, and Cluff had taken her too much by surprise for her to rearrange it properly. She had not been big earlier in the day at the police-station but he saw her smaller now, dried-up, withered with conflicting emotions amongst which sorrow was the least. Brown shadows underlined eyes flecked with red. Her pinched lips and her cheeks alike lacked colour. She wore older clothes than when he had last seen her, long accustomed to preserving such finery as she could afford for her excursions into the streets.

Clive pressed against his leg. Cluff missed nothing of the room's appearance, too small by far for the three of them, father, mother, daughter. A worn armchair, its upholstery frayed into holes, leaking wisps of stuffing, faced its equally decrepit twin across the hearth, both relegated in their age from once-proud occupancy of the front parlour. An open fire, low, needing fuel, sulked in a high grate, part of a range that included an oven on one side and a hot-water boiler on the other. Coconut matting, trodden into strands, covered the floor, showing through its tears patches of flaking, stone flags. A stained cloth hid the top of a table against the rear wall, between the door to the passage and a door into the pantry under the stairs. A chair at the side of the table nearest the little scullery, its outer wall at right-angles to the living-room window, fronted a newspaper spread on the tablecloth. A pint mug, a knife, a fork, and a spoon were arranged on the paper.

He could hear music, not near but providing a background to the atmosphere of the room. If the exterior walls of these houses were thin those dividing them inside were thinner. Nothing that happened in any room of this house would go unheard in another, or fail to have its meaning interpreted. Where was privacy for the people living in it? How could they get away from each other? How could they bridge, in surroundings like these, the gap between the generations?

She heard the music as well, cheerful, its beat quick, anything but funereal. She looked hard at the wall containing the fireplace. She said, "They don't care. She wasn't their child."

"I don't blame her for the money," Cluff thought, the notes in the daughter's wallet heavy against his thigh. "She'd a right to get away from this if she could. She didn't ask to be born into it. Was she to sit down and bear it? Better to fight back than to accept and wail. Better to die using the weapons she had than go on miserable and broken."

The mother observed him, clandestinely, ready to glance away if he caught her at it. The absence of the father made him wonder. He felt as sorry for the father as for the daughter, more sorry because the daughter at least had made her escape and the father had no refuge. Cowardice conditioned the father to suffering; the circumstances of his existence forced him into hopelessness.

Cluff searched his memory. His gaze wandered the room seeking to support recollection by tangible evidence. He could see no signs that children were a part of this household. He could not remember that Jane Trundle had ever had brothers or sisters.

In spite of the close, fetid smell, the lack of ventilation, he began to realize that his first impressions were due to the poverty of the house not to the slovenliness of the housewife, another nail in the cross borne by the husband. The stains on the tablecloth were stains that no amount of washing had been able to efface, the newspaper an attempt to prevent more. The holes in the chairs had been darned until the material at their edges would no longer hold thread firm. The stone floor under the matting was swept and clean. The range shone, blackleaded, the handle of its oven mirrorlike. A precision, an order, raised an ugly head from below the surface appearance, compulsive in the woman, the harder to bear because not by the wildest stretch of imagination could it succeed in improving the house one iota. He could see the woman, as her frustration grew, placing more emphasis and more upon dusting and polishing, the house her god not her husband, her husband cared for less and less, subordinated to her new divinity. The mantelpiece was innocent of pipes. Neither ashtrays nor boxes of matches, nor spills of folded paper, lay anywhere about. Whatever smells made up the atmosphere Cluff breathed they did not include the scent of tobacco.

His sympathy for the father increased. Instead of regretting the father he was pleased that he had avoided the father. He had a picture of the father clearly enough in his mind without the need for more detail. He visualized the long misery of the father, deprived of even the poor comforts within reach of his pocket, badgered, brow-beaten, no master, no man. He saw the father, his life empty except for his daughter, the father's heart breaking at the hostility between the women he had to live with, the father compelled to partisanship, unable to run with the hare and hunt with the hounds, digging for himself a deeper pit whatever part he took. There had been no love here except the love of father for daughter and that resented, crushed, until in the end how could it be reciprocated?

The Sergeant had to say something. He couldn't go on standing there, like a statue, a man bewitched. He had already what he had come to learn and he needn't have come because he had known it before, sparing himself the task of redoubling certainty. He sought for an explanation, an excuse however vague, to justify his visit, ill at ease with a pity that embraced both murderer and victim. He did not have to listen to them in Gunnarshaw to know what they were saying, to stand on the kerb and hear their voices as they went by him, to go into the shops or the offices or the public houses. They had something to talk about and let them make the most of it. "It's her own fault," they would be saying, puritan, moral, upright in character and beliefs like this woman with him. "You could see what she was. The way she dressed. Her boldness. Her brazen flaunting of her body."

They had seen only one side of the picture. They hadn't seen this. Who was the victim, the girl for getting herself killed or the man who had killed her? In the excitement of the moment Gunnarshaw marked only the provocation she must have given, the manner in which she'd led some poor devil on until he didn't know whether he was coming or going, until he'd done what he did and passed the point of no return. But what was black and what was white? Where was the pan that could call the kettle black?

Cluff got a hold on himself. He said, "I've been talking to Jack Carter."

The woman's face twisted, sneering, hostile, but Carter wasn't the cause of it. Carter merely emphasized the final blow to her prized respectability, Carter the one hope her daughter might have had thrown to the winds.

"He was too good for her," the woman replied. "He'd have let her walk over him. She could have wiped her feet on him and he wouldn't have complained."

Uninvited, Cluff sat down in one of the armchairs. Clive lay at his feet. His arm dangled, his hand touching the dog's head.

The woman continued, her voice lower, her eyes looking up at the ceiling, listening, "I tried to tell him what she was."

"Who?" Cluff thought. "Your husband or Carter?" He knew where the father was, up there on his bed, nursing his grief in solitude, unable to share with his wife either grief or joy.

"If he'd killed her," the woman said spitefully, "no one could blame him. But he didn't kill her. Not Jack. He worshipped the ground she walked on. He'd still have taken her, shoddy and sec-ondhand as she'd let herself become."

The Sergeant's eyes met the woman's eyes. She dropped hers, outmatched. She asked, "Do you think I didn't know?"

"Men?"

"A daughter of mine—"

"Which men?"

"Oh, she was clever! Would she have told me that? When could I get anything out of her?"

He didn't want her to go on. He said, "Did she come in at all last night?"

"Wait! I'll show you."

His face revealed nothing. Her movements upstairs were violent, noisy. She wrenched open drawers and banged them back, hurling them shut. She stamped her feet and dashed furniture aside until the ceilings shook. Her husband did not call out to her.

She held a snapshot in her hand, blown up to postcard size. She hissed at Cluff, "What's the use of pretending? You'll find out for yourself if you haven't done already." She stabbed the snapshot at him.

The girl posed against a groyne, on a sandy beach, half-turned to the camera, laughing, her eyes provocative. A brassiere hardly hid the swelling of her breasts, the cleft between them deep and tantalizing, the nipples pointed against the cloth. She paraded her round, white belly, dimpled with a neat navel. Nothing else except a triangular band of material, thin, tied tight, gaping over her hips, broke the nakedness of her flesh.

Cluff studied the picture. White houses, shaded by exotic-looking trees, formed a background. The light was sharp and clear and brilliant, the sky cloudless, the sea glinting, the beach a rash of striped umbrellas and canvas backrests on the sand, of bodies next door to nudity, men and women alike.

"She didn't know I'd seen it," the mother said. "She kept it hidden away. She couldn't fool me. I knew where to look."

"It's not in England," Cluff murmured.

"She'd bigger ideas than that. A week at Blackpool wouldn't have done for her."

"It costs money to travel."

"I wasn't hard on her. Only for her own good—"

He wondered how the mother measured, what scale the mother had for good.

He said, "Only a girl —"

"A—" the mother began and managed to stop herself. A trace of fear haunted her stony eyes. The little by which she had escaped revealing to Cluff the full count of her envy and her longing calmed her. She bit back the epithet on the tip of her tongue. She returned to the question Cluff had asked before she left the room. "Earlier than usual," she told him. "In and out as she always did. Prinked and painted and powdered. Dressed like a street-walker."

"With Carter?"

"What are you saying?"

The fire in the grate was no more than a tiny heap of blackening ash, the room cold, without comfort, like the woman he sat with.

"What time?"

For a moment she was far away.

"Try to remember."

"No later than six. I wouldn't dare to ask at the shop. I'd be afraid of what I might hear. I never expected she'd keep her job as long as she did."

Cluff fidgeted, feeling dirty for listening to her.

"She behaved as she liked."

He prepared to get up. Something in her nailed him to his seat.

"I'd no help from her," the woman complained, switching to self-pity. "She left me to do everything. I'm not as young as I was."

"She worked," Cluff said.

"Work! That! She came in at all hours of the night. She lay in bed in the mornings. If she'd had a lock on the door of her room she'd have shut me out."

"I'm not married," Cluff said. "I've no children of my own."

"You're lucky. You don't know how lucky you are."

Cluff neither agreed nor disagreed.

She said, "He never corrected her. He always gave way to her. He left it all to me. I warned him when she was a child. I told him over and over again what he was doing. I said she'd come to a bad end. I knew all along this would happen."

Cluff looked past her, slack in the chair, face still expressionless, unsurprised. The doorway into the passage framed the husband, the father, swaying, ghastly. His head trembled above the open neckband of his shirt. His bony chest was hairless. He hadn't delayed to put on his trousers. Thick, woollen drawers encased bowed legs, tucked at the ankles into socks moist with sweat. How long had he been there? His eyes flamed with a knowledge of his wife's ultimate treachery. She had destroyed the last barriers against the flare of their mutual hatred.

Cluff climbed to his feet, a mourner at the death of a marriage that could not be broken while they lived, because this was Gunnarshaw and they lived in Rupert Street and were middle-aged and had to exist, both of them, on the pittance the man earned, because, more than anything, they were respectable and the wife could not tolerate, if the husband could, what the neighbours would say. The man could no longer deceive himself about the extent of his wife's disloyalty. Everything between them was finished and had to go on still, as it had always done.

"Go back to bed," Cluff advised softly.

He walked slowly across the floor and the man moved back, against the panelling enclosing the stairs, to let him pass. He saw the man's eyes and he put his hand momentarily on the man's arm, the lightest of touches. Clive followed him along the passage and the man had nothing, not so much as a dog.

He let himself out into Rupert Street, the house silent behind him. He closed the door. The cool wind blew on his face and he was grateful for it.

He looked down at the photograph, clutched in his fingers. She smiled up at him in the dim gas-light. This was Rupert Street. She wasn't Rupert Street. Couldn't Carter, who was Rupert Street and Charles Street rolled into one, have seen it? Had Carter so little sense that he set himself to reach for the stars?

# CHAPTER VI

H E TOOK THE TOWPATH INSTEAD OF TURNING DOWN CHARLES Street to the road.

The mill was far behind him. It was accident, more than intention, that he happened to be returning towards the centre of the town. The gable ends of the rows of houses alternated with the spaces that marked in turn the yards at their backs and the grass-grown, weedy streets at their fronts. Curtained windows glowed, the yards on to which they looked palely suffused with their light. Occasionally a back door opened, patching the dark more brilliantly. Shovels scraped in coal-places. The tread of people visiting the outside lavatories rang hollow on stone, accompanied by the flush of cisterns. Now and again snatches of voices reached his ears, the complaining tones of a woman, a man's angry exclamation, the wail of an infant, the startled cry of a child assaulted for some peccadillo.

He could not see where he was putting his feet, the path dark, no light falling on it, the gables of the rows blank. He walked surely despite the darkness and the puddles, the potholes hollowed by weather and neglect, not hesitant or stumbling, his feet confident in the manner of his ancestors bred to the roughness of the moors.

In the shadows ahead the shadow of Clive ranged. A whiteness on the black water revealed itself, as Cluff came abreast, a swan, still, alerted by the dog, watchful. He could not recall ever having seen a swan on the canal before. It pleased him and he stayed by it for some time, speculating on its origin, the reason for its being there, its probable destination.

A swing-bridge to his left led from a break in the embankment to a farm track on the opposite bank. Beyond the bridge, on his right, the shuttered bunkers of another mill frowned on him. A tall chimney soared above the bulk of weaving-sheds, tapering, its top invisible.

There were buildings now on both banks, parallel with the banks, their walls fencing the towpath on this side and the edge of the canal on the other. A second swing-bridge joined the split trace of a paved road. Lights blazed in the windows of a hospital. The canal widened into a basin, overhung by the cowled hoods of loading bays, a couple of cranes poking their jibs over the water. Two or three ships' lifeboats, converted into the semblance of cabin cruisers, top-heavy and unwieldy, moored against a concrete wharf. A cow in the holding-shed of the town slaughter-house bawled suddenly and briefly.

The canal narrowed, going under a stone bridge. The towpath sloped almost level with the water. His feet echoed and he had to bend his head to avoid the curved stonework. On the other side of the bridge he climbed, reluctantly, the worn treads of steps mounting to the street.

It must have been later than he had thought, his progress up the canal bank slow and interspersed by his frequent stops. The shops were closed, the traffic on the road sparse, people on the pavements few. In the distance a road junction, with a traffic island in the middle, marked the meeting of the road he was on with two others.

He wandered on, his brain woolly with half-formed impressions, which he made no attempt to clarify or catalogue. He stopped at the junction, faced with the alternative of turning left into the High Street or right along the main road that would bring him to the outskirts of Gunnarshaw on the south. He thought of his car in the High Street, and of Barker. He took the road, crossing at the island, choosing to walk on the darker pavement, away from the bright, deserted foyer of a cinema, red neon letters shining on its façade above the glass porch sheltering its entrance.

He walked a long way and went to the other side of the road and came back until he could see the lights of the cinema again in front of him. Instead of passing it he turned into a side-road, plunging into a maze of unadopted hilly streets. Lights in the window of a corner shop astonished him a little. He went closer and the smell of cooked food stirred his empty stomach. Clive moved eagerly about his legs, letting him know that the dog had not fed either since breakfast.

He pushed a glass-panelled door between shop windows made opaque to more than half their height with brown paint. The place was hardly a café, converted from some other trade, most of its business the sale of ready-cooked food to millworkers and wives who went on working after marriage. They left their plates and basins in the morning and collected their pies and stews at noon. The prices were cheap and the food appetizing.

Occasional customers ate in the shop. It stayed open late at night, missing no chances of profit. A few round tables crowded together in front of the counter at the back of the room. A tea urn perched at one end of the counter, flanked by a plate of cakes, not many cakes and not fancy cakes because the people of Gunnarshaw preferred more substantial food and called no meal a meal unless it involved the use of a knife and fork. Feathers of steam escaped from the urn, which grumbled and squeaked, sotto voce, to itself. Placards on the wall listed the humble prices of humble dishes, pies and peas, sausages and mash, bacon and eggs, meat and potato pie.

A girl leaned her head on her hands, her elbows on the counter. She wasn't busy. Dumpy and plain, her face shone and her eyes twinkled. The bell on the door jangled as Cluff and Clive came in. She straightened and looked up, pleased to have company. Her smile faded a little when she saw Cluff. She couldn't quite make up her mind whether she'd wanted Cluff or not.

He sat down and unbuttoned his coat. She approached him warily, her eyes fixed on his face.

"It's me, Doris," Cluff said. "I'm not a ghost."

She stopped before she reached the table. She continued to look at him.

"I'm not in a hurry if you're not," Cluff said.

Whatever her thoughts were they didn't hide the laughter that lived in her eyes, the humour round the corners of her mouth. A man could forget she wasn't pretty because she was jolly.

"I might have known," she said ruefully, mocking herself. "There's no getting away from you."

Cluff stared at her for a while. She stared back at him, wrinkling her nose. "Bring something for the dog," Cluff told her. "You can say what you have to say later."

"And you, Sergeant?"

"You might as well, now I'm here."

"It's the first time."

"You're off my usual track."

"You don't know what you've been missing."

"Anything. I don't care what."

Clive's lips smacked over a well-filled dish on the floor. Cluff looked a little dubiously at a steaming pie surrounded by a moat of pale-green peas. She sat with him at the table.

"Go on," the girl invited. "I know there's a barber next door, but he's not called Sweeney Todd."

He dug the end of his knife into the crust and levered the blade down. Gravy spurted to inundate the peas. She pushed a bottle of sauce across to him. "Wait a minute," she said and left him to draw two cups of tea from the urn.

She held the cup to her lips. "Well," she said. "Get it over with. Don't tell me. I know what I ought to have done."

"Get what over with?" Cluff asked, through a mouthful of peas.

"The lecture."

"We'll skip the lecture."

"The trouble is," she said, "he's such a harmless sort of a chap. A puff of wind would blow him away."

"That's right."

"We must be getting popular," Doris remarked, looking round the room.

Cluff, reloading his fork, replied, "I'll give you a recommendation anyway."

"The 'Crown's' more in her line than a spot like this," she added. "Mind you, she brightened the place up. I'd give my right arm to look like her."

"You'll do as you are."

"Safer, I'll say that."

Cluff applied himself to the task of balancing peas.

"I'd have got around to coming," Doris said. She corrected herself, "At least, I'd have kept a lookout for you."

"It's funny," Cluff murmured. "Usually I hear more than I want to know. This time people don't seem to want to tell me anything." He paused. "Not people like you."

"I'm no different from most others in Gunnarshaw."

"I know."

He cleaned his plate: "I don't see what you're worried about. She's dead and you're not."

"She'd something to look back on, I'll bet."

"You've something to look forward to."

"I'm still hoping."

Cluff pushed his plate away. Clive sat back, licking his chops.

"Have another," Doris suggested.

"I think I will. They're good."

She put his plate down, refilled: "I'll feel better when you're fed."

"Where did you learn that?"

"At our house it's food first and talk afterwards."

"You couldn't do better," Cluff said, chewing.

"Will they hang him?"

Cluff went on eating.

"They shouldn't. I wouldn't have thought he had it in him."

Cluff didn't reply.

"He looked just like a pup that's lost its mother." She considered. "How did he manage to get hold of her? It doesn't work the other way round."

"Eh?"

"My way. I can't catch anything in trousers. It's not for want of trying."

"I'm here."

"Yes," Doris said, looking down her nose. "We all know how fond of women you are."

He put his knife and fork down and sat back.

"Men haven't much sense. If he would bring her in here what could he expect?"

"His name isn't Rockefeller."

"Say that again!"

He glanced at a yellow-faced clock ticking loudly on the wall: "You didn't happen to notice the time?"

"About seven. You should have heard her."

"You did."

"All right, I was listening. One look at them and you would have done too."

"It's my job."

"I could have slapped her myself."

"Well?"

"They were wet. You know what sort of a night it was. He kept talking about the pictures but she wasn't keen. She asked him, 'In the one-and-threes?'"

"It would have been."

"I wouldn't have minded the chance. I could have hit him as well, for not standing up to her."

Cluff pulled the photograph he had brought with him from Rupert Street out of his pocket. He asked, "Are you sure? This girl?"

Doris pursed her lips and whistled: "I'd be an eyeful in one of those. Of course I'm sure."

Cluff put the photograph away.

"Gunnarshaw won't look the same without her," Doris said.

"Nothing's what it was."

"In the end," Doris said, "she got up and left him. They'd been talking in whispers. I couldn't hear much once they lowered their voices. But I could see their faces, his white and hers with a look on it as if he smelt. I managed to catch one or two words. He told her, 'I'm getting a raise next month.' She stared at him and laughed."

"But he stayed after she'd gone?" Cluff pressed her, hopefully.

"Hold on! I didn't say so. He threw half-a-crown on the table and ran out after her without waiting for his change."

Cluff sighed. Doris went behind the counter. She came back with a fraying scarf in her hand: "He was in so much of a hurry he forgot this."

"He hasn't lost much."

"I suppose you'll want it."

"I don't see what option I have."

She looked at him closely: "I haven't told anyone."

"You've told me."

"Not anything you didn't know?"

He answered the plea in her voice by shaking his head. He said, "What I didn't know I could guess. You couldn't have kept it to yourself."

She stood by his chair, doubtful. She insisted, "It was me you came to see?"

"I was passing."

Her sense of humour got the better of her anger: "I've done it, haven't I?"

He finished his cup of tea: "How much do I owe you?"

She totted up his bill and told him.

He walked more rapidly, back to the High Street and up the road to the police-station. It occurred to him that during the whole of his conversation with Doris neither he nor she had mentioned Jack Carter by name. He'd assumed she meant Carter and she'd assumed that he knew who she was talking about. It needn't have been Carter. Was Carter the only man in Gunnarshaw? He knew quite well it was Carter. There was no other man in Gunnarshaw it could have been.

An excited Barker confronted him in the outer office.

Barker said, "I didn't know where you'd got to. I've been ringing the cottage."

"Annie's not still there?"

"I couldn't get any reply."

"Good. It's safe to go home then."

"I knew you were still in Gunnarshaw. Your car—"

"My car?"

"Don't you remember? I drove it in this morning."

"So you did."

Barker trailed him into his office. "Listen," he said, "I've—"

Inspector Mole poked his head round the door, interrupting Barker. Mole commented to Cluff, "You're back." He asked, without any confidence, "How's it going?"

Cluff sat down in his chair. Barker hopped on the other side of the table, bursting with news. Mole, refusing to accept that he wasn't wanted, made no move to leave them alone.

Barker couldn't contain himself any longer. Mole or no Mole he had to say, "I've got the surgeon's report. She was going to have a baby."

"Well, well, well!" Mole said, emphasizing each word.

Cluff dragged a scarf from somewhere about his person. He placed it on the table.

"It didn't show," Mole commented.

"Two to three months," Barker elucidated.

Cluff said, "I don't believe it." Barker stared at him, thunderstruck.

"I shouldn't argue with our surgeon," Mole advised. "He doesn't take quietly to contradiction even when he's only expressing an opinion. He'll have something more than an opinion to go on."

"It's true," Barker asserted, thinking that Cluff was accusing him of having made a mistake.

Mole interrupted, in his official voice, "That just about buttons it up. That and the letter."

"So you'd read the letter?" Cluff said.

"Naturally. You must have heard by now who 'Jack' is."

"I've known all along who he is."

"Then it's simple."

"Everybody knows," Cluff said. "Jack Carter."

"Everybody—?"

"In Gunnarshaw."

"I didn't know." Mole glared first at Cluff and then at Barker, as if they had been keeping information from him.

"The money—" Cluff said.

"The money?" The money was no problem to Mole. "Blackmail. The letter reeks of panic—"

"Or despair."

"—Fear in every line of it. No wonder. The baby explains everything."

"Don't you know Carter?"

"We aren't all Gunnarshaw men."

"He hasn't any money."

"He'd that much anyway."

"She had it."

"It's clear enough where she got it from. Where's he work? You've only got to dig around a bit. I didn't say he'd come by it honestly."

Cluff wasn't paying any attention. He stared at Barker and Mole without seeing either of them. Instead of Barker and Mole he saw her father. He heard her father repeating, "She was a good girl," the father's futile self-deception: "I trusted her." No one could keep this from her father. When a girl died as she'd died death was public property.

Cluff slumped in his chair. "I can't believe it," he said a second time and saying it made him more certain that he was right.

He could believe it of Jack Carter, of Jack Carter in love, of any youth in love, his love returned. He couldn't believe it of Jane Trundle, not with Jack Carter, not as careless as that even if her rejection of him had only been a sham. Carter penniless, a life with Carter the duplicate in time of the life she lived in Rupert Street, she and Carter the inevitable repetition in the future of her mother and father, the same poverty, the same dinginess and decay and eternal cheeseparing. It didn't fit. Her pregnancy made it all the more unlikely.

He emptied his pocket, Carter's crumpled letter begging her to meet him, the wallet with the money, her photograph. He placed the photograph on the table, meticulously, setting it exactly to rights until its position satisfied him. Mole moved round the table and leaned over it, much taken by the photograph.

"Not with Carter," Cluff told himself, again and again. "Not with Carter." She knew too much. She'd seen too much. There was more in those eyes than provocation, or promiscuous invitation.

He had it now. Calculation. Beautiful, but beautiful in the manner of a work of art, cold like a statue, with no emotions, no warmth of feeling, no possibility of surrendering herself, all else forgotten, to the passion of the moment.

He couldn't envisage her in love at all. She'd had too much experience, with the example of her parents in front of her, of love. She wasn't capable of love, even if love could be accompanied by wealth and position. For her to have loved Carter, for a single instant, was impossible. How could Carter have paid for her body? She'd no other asset, nothing else to trade with. She knew where she was going, away from Rupert Street, and nothing Carter could have done or said would have been instrumental in turning her from the object she had set herself.

"A baby," Cluff thought, sure that with her a baby, too, would be part of her plan, another weapon she'd armed herself with, deliberately, something the father, whoever he was, couldn't repudiate. The Sergeant's arm moved and it sent the scarf sliding. Mole grabbed at the scarf and missed. The scarf slid to the floor and Cluff put his foot on it.

He wasn't worried about the scarf, about the quarrel Carter had had with her in the eating-house. The letter Carter had written to her could be ignored. What was it to Cluff that she had walked away from the chemist's arm-in-arm with Carter, Greensleeve watching them, and Margaret and Jean, that she had met Carter again later that evening after a brief visit to Rupert Street and dismissed him with a finality he wouldn't accept?

Barker coughed. Mole, with the photograph still in view, had forgotten the scarf already. Cluff's heart grew heavier. His eyes almost closed. After all, it didn't follow. There was a fallacy in his argument. If he rejected the quarrel and the letter and Carter's pursuit of her, couldn't he reject equally the money in her wallet, her pregnancy, the certainty he had of her character? Was this set of facts more valid than the other? Which coincidence, running parallel to the truth but apart from it, which of the two the one to be set aside? He knew her. He knew Carter as well. Carter insulted beyond endurance, withered by her scorn, as unstable and emotional as she was stable and frigid. A would-be lover, with no hope left, unprepossessing, too much aware, even without her confirmation, of his deficiencies, hated not loved, not hated despised, himself, his environment, his family, everything that surrounded him, everything he stood for, which he couldn't change, because it wasn't in him to change anything.

Carter, and all the Sergeant had to do was what Mole expected him to do, and Gunnarshaw, ranging the evidence against Carter until Carter couldn't deny it, until Carter had no loophole left, opportunity and motive unanswerable. What was Carter to Cluff? What were people to the Sergeant?

Someone was speaking. An envelope waved under his nose. Cluff looked automatically at the table, for the envelope containing Carter's letter, and the envelope was still there. The envelope in Barker's hand was a different envelope, newer, whiter, unaddressed, its flap untorn, not sealed down.

The words he could hear were Barker's words and Barker hadn't finished yet. The news Barker had brought so proudly wasn't enough for Barker. He had to drive it home, to emphasize it, to drum it into Cluff until it became the salient fact, the one thing that couldn't be pushed into the recesses of Cluff's mind.

"There's something else—" Barker was saying.

The envelope, the other envelope, tipped. A few shreds of black, brittle matter, minute, speckled the space on Cluff's blotter Barker had cleared. Mole was asking, without interrupting his study of Jane Trundle's picture, "What is it?"

"Her clothes," Barker said. "I'd nothing else to do. I thought—. They'd taken them off at the mortuary. It was easier when she wasn't wearing them—"

Cluff rolled the dry threads between his fingers, feeling them rasp and give against his skin.

"In her shoes," Barker stammered, feeling that he was making a fool of himself. Mole managed at last to free himself from the spell of the snapshot. He glared at Barker angrily, his eyes accusing Barker of further complication, irrelevant, a red herring.

"Caught in the crack between the half-sole and the upper, under the arch," Barker succeeded in elaborating.

Mole asked incredulously, "Don't you believe what's staring you in the face either?"

Cluff leapt to his feet. He snatched at the hat he had thrown carelessly amongst his papers. He was halfway to the door already, Clive in front of him scratching at the threshold. Barker caught him up in the outer office. Mole shouted, "Have you gone mad?" He rushed in his turn through Cluff's door. He yelled, "It could have been there for weeks, whatever it is."

In the street Cluff panted, to Barker, "Thank God there's been no rain to mean anything. If only he's true to character—"

Barker hadn't the slightest idea what he meant.

The chemist's shop was dark. The shops on either side of it were dark, the doors in the High Street, except those of the public-houses, closed. Cluff plunged, without slackening his pace, into a narrow tunnel piercing the line of frontages. He emerged into an open alley not much wider than the tunnel, between cottages that had somehow survived up to the present the planners' mania for destruction. He raced into the road behind the High Street, a few yards along it, and round the corner by the cobbler's, pounding on the setts up to the gate of Greensleeve's yard. He tugged and pulled at the gate.

He said, "It's bolted on the inside."

He made his hands into a stirrup. He hoisted Barker to the top of the gate and Barker hung, silhouetted in the dark, black against a lesser black. The constable vanished, landing with a gasp. Bolts jarred. Cluff hurled himself impatiently at the gate, forcing the leaves inwards. Barker staggered back, almost knocked off his feet.

A torch flashed.

"He didn't," Cluff said with relief. "He didn't!"

The car had gone but the yard hadn't been swilled or swept. Cluff, on his knees, scrabbled at the cracked concrete, his nose to the ground, cursing at Clive to stand away, urging Barker to hold the torch closer.

# CHAPTER VII

"HAS HE BEEN THERE ALL NIGHT?" MARGARET ASKED JEAN. Greensleeve's two remaining assistants came up the High Street together, the street not crowded but comfortably filled with men and women on their way to work, the morning grey and dull like yesterday, the rain still threatening. The clock in the church tower showed a minute or two before nine.

"Why don't you tell him?" Margaret pleaded.

The younger girl objected uncertainly, "But it can't matter. How could it matter? I can't go to him with a thing like that—"

"She's been murdered."

"What would he think of me?" Jean muttered, her eyes on Cluff.

"Worse if you don't."

"It can't have anything to do with it. It can't!"

"You don't know."

"If I was wrong—"

"You weren't wrong."

"I must have been."

"He's no better than anyone else," Margaret said. She wasn't looking at Cluff but at Greensleeve's name above the door of the shop. "I've worked for him longer than Jane did. Has he ever paid any attention to me, or to you?"

"Why don't you like him?"

"Do you?"

"We work there."

"Have you seen his wife lately?"

"It's nothing to do with Jane's death."

"She's never in the town, is she? Do they ever go out together? Would you think he was married at all if you didn't know?"

Cluff's hands were thrust into the pockets of his coat. His hat was pulled forward over his eyes. He had Clive with him.

Margaret said, "He doesn't deserve shielding," not referring to Cluff.

"Couldn't I have made a mistake?"

"You're frightened."

"It isn't that. Our jobs—"

"Greensleeve doesn't run this town, if he thinks so."

"I'd never get another."

"Is that what you're worried about?"

Greensleeve's car appeared on the road by the church. Margaret had her hand on Jean's arm, pulling her gently past the chemist's door in the direction of Cluff, farther away by the fruit-stall in his favourite spot.

The car swung perilously across the roadway, without warning to following traffic. Brakes squealed. A horn blew angrily. The car halted on the setts, its nose pointed at the pavement.

Greensleeve got out. Cluff remained still, his eyes on the flags at his feet, not looking either up the street or down, or at the windows he was facing. He took no notice either of Margaret and Jean, or of Greensleeve. He stood there, big and solid, conspicuous. Greensleeve couldn't ignore him, any more than could the other pedestrians. Everyone in the vicinity was aware of Cluff, the sense of awareness transmitted from one person to another. They left him alone this morning, as they had done yesterday, not trespassing on his remoteness.

Greensleeve stepped forward, cutting Margaret and Jean off from Cluff. They stopped and the expression on Greensleeve's face was difficult to interpret. He glanced over his shoulder at Cluff and when he looked back at the two girls he was smiling. Jean wriggled free from Margaret's grip. She began to cross the pavement in front of Greensleeve. He passed her in the entrance to his shop and inserted a key in the lock. He carried himself straight, with his shoulders pulled back, and Jean thought that he looked just as well as the day before, less preoccupied than for some time past, pleased with himself. He looked round before he went into the shop. He remarked, "The Sergeant's like a horse. I do believe he can go to sleep on his feet." He laughed. "He's stood there so many times and for so long there's quite a hollow in the kerb." Cluff seemed to be in a world of his own, unconnected with the world about him.

Greensleeve wound up the blind that covered the glass panel in the door. He reversed an advertisement card hanging from the top of the door frame, replacing the word "Closed" by "Open." He said, about Cluff, "He'd be better off doing the work he's paid for."

Jean's head turned. She could still see Cluff through the glass in the door. Her own manner had something in it of Cluff's apartness. Like the Sergeant she had forgotten where she was.

"Jean," Greensleeve interrupted her thoughts, but mildly.

She started and flushed. Without meeting his eyes she went through the dispensary to the cloakroom at the back.

"What do you talk about?" Greensleeve wanted to know from Margaret.

She looked at him insolently and went after Jean. He stood for a while by one of the counters, beating a tattoo with his fingers on the glass.

In the street it became quieter, too early yet for housewives on their morning shopping expeditions. The people on the pavements had thinned, by this time being indoors at their desks or mooning in the shops, bored, waiting for customers. The entrances and the pavements had been swept, the night's film of dust flicked from the window displays, perishables brought out of refrigerators and arranged for sale on their slabs. The town had a somnolent air, half returned, after the business of waking, to sleep. It hugged itself close against the cold wind, relaxed in semi-hibernation, its circulation slow.

At the police-station Constable Barker, in his plain clothes, stopped watching the street door. If he'd got out of bed two feet taller because of his unexpected elevation to the post of Cluff's assistant, his elation had evaporated. He left a chair placed near an electric fire and began to move across the outer office. Mole's voice halted him. Mole said silkily, "And where do you think you're off to?"

"Perhaps the Sergeant's been in already."

"What! Didn't he leave you any instructions?"

"He must be in the town somewhere."

"I shouldn't rely on it. He's just as likely to be at that cottage of his."

Barker shook his head.

Mole said, "It'd take more than a mere murder to make Cluff get a move on."

"He's not there. I've rung through."

"Ought we to send out a search-party?"

"I'll find him."

"What happened last night?"

"He went home."

"Is that all?"

Barker, embarrassed, held his lips firmly together.

"All right," Mole said, after a pause. "If you've nothing else to do why don't you see Carter?"

"I haven't been told—"

"I only hope," Mole wished, "it'll stop where it has done. Another murder would be too much when he's only got this far with the first one."

"There's no proof—"

"This is Gunnarshaw. There aren't so many to choose from."

Greensleeve prowled his shop restlessly, the more restlessly as the morning dragged by. He couldn't settle in the dispensary. He found himself missing, as he hadn't done until now, Jane Trundle's presence. A gap yawned between himself and his two assistants. He couldn't feel anything in common with them. He suspected Margaret of digging the gap and Jean of helping her. He hadn't noticed them much while Jane had been there to brighten his days. He couldn't achieve a familiarity with them out of the blue, however much he felt a need to talk.

He paced between the counters, eyeing Jean in charge of the cosmetics, looking out of the other corners of his eyes at Margaret with the patent medicines and baby foods. The outer door drew him like a magnet. As often as he drifted away from it he drifted back. The arrangement of the windows didn't satisfy him. He kept opening and shutting the hatches in the screens that separated the windows from the shop. He altered the position of an article here, of another there. He fiddled with the cardboard props of advertisement cut-outs. He knew very well that Cluff was a few steps away. Cluff had taken on an air of permanency.

Back in the dispensary he heard a knock at the yard door. He looked through the window and motioned the man who had cleaned his car to come in.

The man asked, "Is there anything for me this morning?"

Greensleeve shook his head: "I haven't paid you yet."

"Didn't I do a good job?"

The chemist groped in his trousers' pocket for change. He couldn't find any. He got out his wallet and selected a ten-shilling note. The man's eyebrows lifted and he snatched at the note before it occurred to Greensleeve to alter his mind. The man offered, "Anytime."

He paused on his way out. He advised, "You want to be more careful. You forgot to bolt the gate last night."

"What are you talking about?"

"Anybody could have got in."

"Nonsense!" Greensleeve said. "I remember distinctly. I came back through the shop after I'd got the car out."

"It'd be easier to have a lock fixed so you could shut the gate from outside."

"In any case, it's been left open before." The chemist thought of something. He pushed past his visitor into the passage. He went into the yard and walked over to the gate.

"There's nothing to see," the man said, at his heels.

Greensleeve shrugged it off: "You must have been dreaming."

"I'm in, aren't I?"

"One of the girls—"

"Somebody climbed over, that's a fact," the man added, pointing to the shallow scar of a shoe-toe scraped on the paint.

"Nothing's been touched."

"A kid after a ball, maybe."

"It could have been."

"There's some queer goings-on in Gunnarshaw these days."

"It happens in all kinds of places."

"We're still different. Caleb Cluff doesn't happen everywhere."

"I wouldn't call that a cause for congratulation."

"He seems interested—"

"What in?"

"This shop for one. I suppose he's still at the front?"

"You've seen him then?"

"I like to keep an eye on him if I can. He's got a habit of coming up quietly behind a chap when you don't know he's there."

"You make too much of him. There's nothing extraordinary about Cluff, unless it's his lack of intelligence."

"I watched him yesterday when he left here. He—"

"Left here!" Greensleeve echoed sharply.

"Didn't you know?"

"He was in to see me, certainly."

"Getting on for two. I was just coming back to finish off. I'm not to a few minutes extra on a job for you, Mr. Greensleeve."

Cunning showed on the man's face. He stole a glance at Greensleeve and allowed the seconds to pass. He said, "He came out from the shop." He added, "I always thought you went for your dinner about that time."

"He'd no right—"

"That wouldn't stop Cluff."

"What did he want?"

"Nay," the man replied. "Cluff wouldn't tell that to me."

Greensleeve was turning away.

"He went into yon cobbler's," the man said. "He was in there quite a while."

Greensleeve stopped. He heard, "I wish I'd his job on his pay. He's nowt to do except stroll about and chat with his cronies."

"You can sweep up if you want to."

"Right!"

"I've some cases in the store. Get rid of them for me as well."

"Anything you like." The man stopped Greensleeve in his tracks a second time: "It's a proper spot for a murder this town is. Cluff won't get away with it twice. He was nobbut lucky last time."

Greensleeve stalked into the shop, his step determined. Margaret's eyes followed him to the front door. He hesitated briefly and then went through the door into the High Street, banging the door behind him, setting its bell, suspended from a spring, ringing. Margaret hurried from behind her counter. She peered through the glass door-panel. She said, "He's going up to the Sergeant."

She heard Jean move uneasily. She added, "We don't know what he's telling him."

The chemist hadn't troubled about either a hat or a coat. He came bustling along the pavement. The stall-holder saw him and sidled from one end of his stall to the other, nearer where Cluff continued to ignore everything. The stall-holder's ears pricked. He turned his back to the pavement and began an urgent rearrangement of his piles of fruit.

"What do you think you've been doing?" Greensleeve shouted, before he had come up to Cluff.

He had to halt or run into Cluff. He said, without lowering his voice, "You'd no authority."

Cluff looked up, over the crown of Greensleeve's head. He said quietly, "When?"

The stall-holder abandoned pretence and listened openly.

"I must have been at lunch."

"Oh, then."

Cluff moved a little away. His eyes met those of the stall-holder. They lit up with a brief spark of fire.

"You take too much on yourself," Greensleeve protested.

Cluff fingered an apple. He picked it up and began to roll it in his hand.

Greensleeve threatened, "I've friends on the County Council. I know the chairman of the Watch Committee."

Cluff looked bored.

"You'd no warrant."

"I took the quickest way out for where I wanted to go," Cluff said.

"You've had too much rope in this town."

"You know what to do."

Greensleeve spluttered. He became suddenly conscious of the stall-holder near Cluff's broad back. He might have had a large say in the affairs of Gunnarshaw but he knew he wasn't popular with its humbler citizens. His own class didn't always love him. The stall-holder grinned, enjoying his exchange with Cluff, leaving Greensleeve in no doubt about which side he supported.

Cluff whistled softly to his dog. He began to saunter off, Clive behind him. "Wait!" Greensleeve said loudly. The stall-holder's grin got broader, the stall-holder's manner more contemptuous. The chemist swung round and stamped back to his shop. A passer-by asked the stall-holder, "What's up?"

"He wants taking down a peg," the stall-holder stated.

"The Sergeant's the man to do that."

"Greensleeve's bitten off more than he can chew this time."

"It doesn't pay to tangle with Cluff."

"You wait," the stall-holder prophesied. "Caleb'll show him."

"Steady on. It wasn't him, was it?"

The stall-holder said darkly, "If it wasn't, he knows more than he'll let on."

Greensleeve ignored Margaret. He walked up to Jean and accused her, "Why didn't you let me know he came back when I was out yesterday?"

Margaret smiled.

"I was by myself," Jean said.

"You let him into the dispensary."

"He left the back way." Jean hesitated, nervous. "He wasn't here for long."

"Why?"

"I'd hardly time to talk to him."

Greensleeve looked at the younger girl for what seemed to her a long time. "You're telling the truth?" he said, and she nodded. His eyes narrowed. He added, "You've a pleasant job here. I pay you well," and went into the dispensary, closing the door after him.

He stood, thinking. Through the window he could see the man from the rag-merchant's brushing the yard languidly, with longer intervals between each stroke. The chemist remembered the mockery in the stall-holder's face, the innuendo he had imagined in the remarks of the man in the yard when they were discussing Cluff.

He made up his mind. He searched quickly through the pages of a directory. He lifted the phone, dialled the exchange, and asked for the number he wanted.

Margaret had her ear to the dispensary door. "He's phoning," she said to Jean.

"Please," Jean begged.

"You're a fine one to talk."

"I didn't come back that night intentionally."

Margaret moved away from the dispensary door: "If you say so. You'd only be telling the Sergeant what he suspects already."

"How could he?"

"Has he been standing out there for nothing?"

Jean looked away.

"He'll find out," Margaret said. "You know what they say about him in Gunnarshaw. He hears everything sooner or later."

"If I cause trouble—"

"What's he going to think about you if you don't go to him first?"

Cluff walked with his head down and his shoulders hunched, keeping a straight course. The people he met moved aside to let him pass.

He hadn't lived so long in Gunnarshaw without having a good idea of which of its three banks to go into. A door opposite to him across the floor as he entered was lettered "Manager." He spoke to a cashier behind a grille on his left. The cashier disappeared round a wooden screen hiding the pedestrian activities of the bank. Spurning a chair, Cluff perched on a table, turning the pages of a pamphlet he took from the top of a pile of pamphlets, about facilities for loans to farmers.

The door of the Manager's office opened. The Manager's bald head craned forward. He peered nearsightedly through thick spectacles, fixing Cluff's position. He beckoned and Cluff told Clive to stay where he was.

"What can I do for you, Sergeant?" the Manager asked.

"These," Cluff replied and laid on the Manager's desk the bundle of notes from Jane Trundle's handbag.

"It's hardly regular," the Manager said doubtfully.

"I wouldn't ask without a good reason."

"As it's you," the Manager agreed.

"They're new. They're new issue."

The Manager picked them up to confirm for himself what Cluff said. He offered, without inquiring the precise nature of Cluff's visit, "I might be able to help. To the extent at least of tracing their first withdrawal." He was a very correct man. "Within limits," he made it clear. "If they came from us."

"They did," Cluff said, hoping it was true.

"Then we'll know the cashier. But it's not often a customer withdraws in hundreds at a time. We do much of our business over the counter in small transactions, five pounds here, ten there." He warmed to his subject. "It's not easy to let you know who gets each separate pound note. If they'd been of higher denominations now. Our system—"

"Do your best," Cluff both interrupted and urged.

A little regretful the Manager pushed the button of a bell on the side of his desk. He issued detailed and lengthy instructions to the clerk who appeared immediately.

They chatted, Cluff's brief, monosyllabic answers soon exhausting the subject of murder. The Manager asked after Cluff's relations and reminisced about an older generation of Cluffs. The writing of a local history ought to have been well within his capacity.

The clerk returned, accompanied by the Chief Cashier. The Chief Cashier laid a sheet of paper on the Manager's desk. It contained a list of names with pencilled figures beside each one. The Chief Cashier and the Manager held a whispered consultation. The Manager dismissed the Cashier with a curt word of thanks.

The Manager, not without a sense of atmosphere, leaned back in his chair, postponing elucidation. Cluff, knowing his man, didn't hurry him. The Manager surrendered first. He pushed the paper at Cluff and stared over the rims of his glasses, which had slipped down to the tip of his nose. "That's the best we can do, Sergeant," he said, smug with achievement.

Cluff glanced at the paper. He pushed it back to the Manager. The Manager took it up and tore it in half. He arranged the halves together and divided the result. He proceeded in a similar fashion until the task was beyond the strength of his fingers and allowed the confetti he had made to trickle downwards into his wastepaper basket. He remarked, "If it had been anyone but you I'd have required an authority."

"Nothing of this will come out."

"Exactly."

How much did it mean, Greensleeve's name amongst a dozen names?

Clive barked a greeting as he came with Cluff out of the bank. A despondent Barker put out a hand to stroke the dog. "I'd forgotten about you," Cluff said.

"The Inspector wanted me to see Carter."

"You didn't?"

Barker shook his head.

"Why should you?" Cluff asked. He added, "Why shouldn't you?"

The moors rose high above the roofs of the buildings about them. They could see the houses of an estate climbing the slopes, a witness in a way to Greensleeve's energy and ambition, each house identical with its neighbour, identically painted by council law, dogs not permitted by order of Greensleeve, gardens to be kept clean and tidy, lodgers prohibited. They deserved what they got, the people who lived there. What had happened to Englishmen?

The estate was like a scar on the side of the moor, red brick not grey stone, its roofs tiled not slated, the petty result of petty men's imaginings. A brown knife-cut above the estate disappeared into a plantation of pines, coming into view again at right-angles to its original course where the trees ceased, threading the flank of the moor just below its crest, where the moor and the sky joined.

"It's a long time since I was up there," Cluff said.

"You can get a car as far as the trees," Barker told him.

"This weather, or in summer?"

"Farther in summer."

Cluff stared, deep in thought.

Barker said, "I'm surprised he risked it."

"Are you sure he did?"

"But aren't you?"

"I'm not sure of anything," Cluff replied. "What did she get out for? What was she doing up there with him, instead of Carter? If she was up there. If he was up there."

Barker suggested, "A gesture? A dramatic gesture?"

"It began in the shop," Cluff thought aloud. "It continued when she took Carter's arm and walked away with him. But why meet him again and leave him again?" He admitted, "You could be right. I can see her doing that. Opening the car door, stepping out, pretending to ignore the rain, the place they were in—'Very well. If that's how it's going to be, I'll walk back.'"

"She wouldn't have done."

"No. She wouldn't have done. But she could make a man think so." Cluff struck the pavement with his stick. "He wouldn't kill her," he said.

"I can't imagine it either. Not a public figure like him."

"I mean Carter, not Greensleeve."

Cluff turned in his tracks. He crossed the road, trailed by Barker and Clive, both Barker and Clive feeling neglected and out of touch with the Sergeant. He walked faster than Barker, with an unusual distaste for the streets, making for the police-station not because it attracted him, but because it provided the most immediate refuge. He yearned for solitude, to be alone not so that he could think but to vegetate peacefully, emptying his mind, waiting for the blank to be filled again by the due process of growth.

His hopes proved vain. The door of his office was closing when Barker and Clive, outdistanced, came into the police-station. The constable on the desk, doing Barker's old job, was on his feet, harassed. He complained to Barker, "I tried to tell him. C.I.D. Headquarters wants him to call. He wouldn't stop to listen."

"Give them a ring and put them through," Barker said. He opened Cluff's door and let himself and the dog in. He informed Cluff, "The Superintendent's coming on the line."

The Sergeant muttered inaudibly. Clive went to lie in his customary position. Barker, not dismissed, shut the door and went to stand by the window.

Cluff told the receiver, "It's me."

"I've been trying to get you," Patterson's voice replied.

"I'll send a report when I'm ready."

"You've put me in a spot."

Cluff snorted: "Greensleeve?"

"Yes."

"What's the complaint?"

"Searching his place without a warrant."

"He's exaggerating."

"He's got influence. The papers pay attention to him."

"They should. He owns a majority of shares in the local weekly."

"It won't do, Caleb."

"He's taking it hard."

"He's that kind of man. Touchy about his rights."

"He's no need to be. He doesn't show any consideration in his dealings with others."

"Why, Caleb?"

"She worked for him."

"He's nothing to do with it, surely."

"I'm sick of hearing that. Are you putting him on a pedestal too, and bowing down to worship him?"

The telephone remained silent. Finally it said, "He's old enough to be her father."

Cluff said bitterly, "Has he got you mesmerized as well?"

"It's tricky," Patterson warned.

"If you're not satisfied—"

Patterson ignored Cluff's remark.

The Sergeant said, "He knows something."

"What evidence have you got?"

"It's true all the same."

Each of them waited, one at either end of the line, for the other to speak. Patterson realized that he would wait for ever if he left it to Cluff to break the silence. The Superintendent chose his words carefully: "You were out when I rang earlier. Mole answered the phone."

Cluff knew what was coming.

Patterson continued, "He made out a pretty good case against a man called Carter."

"He would."

"It held water."

"He doesn't know Carter."

After a long pause Patterson asked, "What am I to do about Greensleeve?"

"Nothing."

"It's not as easy as that."

"You can leave it till tomorrow."

"I see."

Cluff put the receiver down, ignoring "Caleb! Caleb, are you there?" as he settled it on its cradle.

Barker swung round from the window as Mole came in. Mole halted just inside the doorway and looked about him very deliberately, pretending not to see Cluff. When his eyes fell on the Sergeant he simulated astonishment.

The Inspector said, "He's here." His announcement misfired. Neither Cluff nor Barker rose to the bait. Mole had to explain, his moment gone, "Carter."

"So you sent for him?"

"I thought Barker was attending to that."

Cluff's fist crashed on to the table: "What do you want to interfere for?"

Mole began to warn, "Just a—," grateful to be interrupted by the entry of a wild-looking Carter. A constable behind Carter grabbed at Carter's sleeve and the youth still eluded him. Mole stepped aside, ready to defend himself if need be. Carter dashed past him for Cluff. "I couldn't stop—" the constable was panting in pursuit.

Cluff ordered, "Leave him alone," and halted Carter with a single look. The constable retreated to the outer office.

Mole, advancing again, demanded, "Are you satisfied? If Barker didn't fetch him he's come of his own free will."

Carter stared at his scarf, rescued from the floor last night and left on Cluff's desk. His breath smelt of beer and his eyes were red and swollen. Barker slid a chair behind his knees. Carter's knees bent and he sat down suddenly. Cluff got up and came round the table to stand beside him.

"I killed her," Carter said.

"If you want to commit suicide don't ask me to help you. Throw yourself under a train or jump in the canal," Cluff retorted.

Cluff rooted in the confusion on his table. He stuck Carter's letter into Carter's face. "You wouldn't dare. A fourteen-year-old girl might have written it. Not a man."

Carter groaned.

"What did you quarrel about?"

"I loved her."

"The more fool you."

Mole interrupted, "Did you give her the baby?"

Barker fought with the screaming youth. "Liar!" Carter yelled, trying to get at Mole. "Liar! Liar! Liar!" He strained against Barker's hold.

Cluff said, "That won't help you, Jack."

Carter's frenzy ebbed. He looked at Cluff, pleading for the truth. He saw the truth in Cluff's face. Tears began to roll down his cheeks and a speck of blood appeared on his lower lip where he had bitten it.

Carter flung at them, "I don't care. I'd still have married her."

Cluff returned to his chair behind the table: "I believe you would."

Mole opened his mouth, saw Cluff glaring at him, and shut it again. Barker leaned forward, poised on the balls of his feet, ready for action if Carter moved.

Carter moaned, "If only she'd told me."

He waited in vain for support.

"I didn't know," Carter said through his tears. "Really, I didn't."

The room stayed quiet.

"I had to talk to her," Carter continued, the silence too much for him. "It was the first time she'd spoken to me for months—"

Seconds passed before Cluff returned, "You said everything in your letter."

Carter's head hung. Carter said, "I thought— When she came out of the shop—When she came up to me—I was glad—"

"Why did you take her home?"

"She wanted to. I waited for her. She promised—"

"You believed her?"

"I haven't got a car," Carter whispered. "Not so much as a bicycle. It was raining. That's why I took her into the café—" He was looking at the scarf. "It didn't matter what she said. She couldn't help it. If I'd known—."

"You followed her."

"I had to."

"Where?"

"The High Street."

"And then?"

"The chemist—Greensleeve—the man she works for—going into the Town Hall. She went in after him."

"And you?"

"I waited."

"The time?"

"About half-past seven."

Barker interrupted, "It's in the post-mortem report. Well after nine the surgeon says. Perhaps nearer ten."

Carter added, in despair, "She didn't come out."

"The back door," Barker said. "Opposite to where she was found."

"Go on," Cluff murmured.

"I can't!"

Mole dared, in a low voice, "A likely story!" Barker moved back to the window, careless of what might happen to Mole. Carter drooped, exhausted, drained of emotion.

"I walked," Carter said. His eyes wandered to each of them in turn. They didn't ask him where. His lips parted in the beginning of a smile. "Isn't that what you expect me to say? No one saw me. I don't know where I went. When I got home they'd all gone to bed."

"Why not?" Cluff agreed. "A night like that. After being with her in the café."

"You don't believe me," Carter said. "It's all lies. I've no witnesses."

"Why haven't you cautioned him?" Mole objected to Cluff.

Cluff picked up the scarf. He handed it to Carter: "It's yours."
Carter's hand reached for it slowly.

"Have you had anything to eat?" Cluff asked. He continued,
"That place you were in two nights ago—"

"No—"

"The girl there's worried about you. Tell her, from me—"

He watched Carter turn slowly round. Carter stumbled, like a
sleepwalker, for the door, the end of the scarf in his hand trailing
on the floor.

Barker stared at the rain, which was beginning to fall heavily,
running in rivulets down the window panes. Mole struggled for
control, breathing quickly. The Inspector moved abruptly in Carter's
wake. He slammed Cluff's door so hard that Barker thought he'd
splintered the wood.

"A boy like that," Cluff said, shaking his head. His eyes met
Barker's. He got up and motioned Barker to follow him.

Barker stood back, uneasy, looking up and down the High Street.
Cluff tried the nearside front door of Greensleeve's car, parked on
the setts in front of the chemist's shop. The door opened. Cluff
remarked, "He wouldn't believe anyone in Gunnarshaw would steal
a car belonging to him." He thrust his head and shoulders inside
and ran his fingers over the floor-mats. He felt down the sides of
the seats. Barker whispered a warning. A hand seized the Sergeant
from behind. Clive growled menacingly.

Cluff jerked his shoulders, freeing himself. He straightened
unhurriedly. "Don't do that," he told Greensleeve. "I'm stronger
than you are."

"First my shop," Greensleeve stuttered. "Now my car!"

"You know why."

"You're a fool."

"I'm not frightened of you," Cluff said, taking Greensleeve's arm. "Patterson's forty miles away. I've nothing to lose. I'd as soon be out of the police force as in it."

"Let me go!"

"Where were you the night before last?"

"If it's the last thing I do—"

"Don't tempt me!"

"You'll regret this for the rest of your days."

"Shall we try it?"

Greensleeve's manner changed: "What's come over you, Sergeant?"

"There's nothing to stop me taking you to the station."

"People are looking at us."

"Let them!"

"Please. Come inside. Can't we discuss this calmly?"

"Well?"

"If you must know—at a council meeting."

"She knew where to find you."

"You're wrong!"

"Where did she wait for you?"

"I don't know what you mean."

"Your memory's not that short."

Greensleeve pulled himself free: "Very well. They were there."

"I know."

"She's dead. Isn't that enough? She worked for me for four years." He paused. "I won't be the one to put a noose round Carter's neck."

Cluff started to walk away, towards the corner by the church. Greensleeve turned to Barker with a look of appeal. Barker dropped his eyes and went past Greensleeve, after Cluff.

Greensleeve stood there. He closed the door of his car and made slowly for his shop. He stopped in the doorway, realizing that Jean and Margaret were staring at him, Margaret grinning, Jean pale-faced and worried. He shook his head as if to clear it of confusion. He said, "We can't allow this to go on," his words measured. "The whole of Gunnarshaw knows the truth. There's no question about who's guilty. If he won't arrest Carter we'll have to find a police-man who will."

He wondered what was the matter with her. He asked Jean, "Are you ill?" She had a hand to her mouth and he quailed under her fixed, wide-open eyes. He began to explain, reasonably, trying to make it clear to her, "There can't be any doubt about it. The way he used to wait for her, her treatment of him. You must have heard. The town's humming with it."

Margaret's grin widened. He could have struck Margaret. He asked himself, "What have I done to her?" He said, "Isn't the impor-tant thing to punish Jane's murderer? It's the only thing." He added, "It's not what she was, what might have happened in her life apart from Carter." He addressed himself exclusively to Jean, Margaret forgotten. "Don't you agree?" he begged.

Jean spun on her feet. She ran blindly into the dispensary. He heard her running across the dispensary to the cloakroom behind. He called after her, "It must be Carter, Jean."

He half-turned, helplessly, to Margaret and he couldn't bear to stay in Margaret's presence. She didn't move until he had gone. Then she strolled to the door, into the shop entrance. Cluff and

Barker, with Clive, stood together in a little group, this side of
the church, opposite the Town Hall on the farther pavement.
Greensleeve hurried, conspicuous in the rain, making an exhibi-
tion of himself that no one in Gunnarshaw, a couple of days ago,
would have credited.

Jean pushed against Margaret, dressed for the street. Jean said
desperately, "How can he talk like that?"

"It isn't true," Margaret goaded. "But if it was true Carter was
driven to it. Where are you going?"

"Must I—?"

"You've got to tell. If Carter killed her, there's an excuse. The
Sergeant can't help Carter unless he knows. No one'll believe what
Carter says on Carter's word alone." She watched Jean. "What
must it be like for Carter? Carter's word against Greensleeve's—"

# CHAPTER VIII

"AGAIN?" CLUFF SAID, FENDING GREENSLEEVE OFF.

"You must have talked to Carter," Greensleeve pleaded.

"You'll catch cold. Where's your coat?"

"She'd go with any man who asked her to."

"You knew her better than I did."

"No—"

"Yes."

"He's a liar if he said so."

"Perhaps not."

"What did he tell you?"

"They were together, Jane and Carter. You saw them—twice."

"You're guessing."

Cluff moved on to the setts, across the road. He began to climb the steps in front of the Town Hall.

Greensleeve held Barker's arm: "Weren't you there? Hadn't Carter found out?"

"Found out?"

"What did he kill her for?"

He couldn't hold Barker any more than he had been able to hold Cluff. He felt eyes watching him from windows. He started back for the shop and saw Jean coming towards him. She lifted her head and turned quickly, her feet pattering away. He ran a few paces and forced himself to a walk, despairing of catching her or, if he caught her, of what he could say in the street. Margaret stood in the entrance to his shop. She moved inside, scornful, back to her place at the counter. He stayed on the threshold, out of the rain.

Cluff came out of the Town Hall and spoke to Barker, who was waiting for him at the bottom of the steps. The two men and the dog recrossed the road. They rounded the corner by the church. Just before the buildings cut off their view down the High Street, Barker looked round.

"Can you see him?" Cluff asked.

"By the shop."

They walked over a bridge.

Barker said, "Gunnarshaw'll never believe it."

"Do you?"

"It's difficult—"

"You're wrong," Cluff said. "Gunnarshaw would be glad to believe it. What friends has he made in Gunnarshaw? The higher they climb the harder they fall."

"Are you certain?"

"It wasn't a long meeting. They make all their decisions in committee. They'd nothing to do except confirm the committees' minutes."

Cluff added, "In any case, he didn't stay to the end."

"It's odd—"

"She wanted him to see her with Carter. Not merely once, when she left the shop. Again, at a place meaning more to him than the shop."

"Carter wasn't with her that time."

"Behind her. Would Greensleeve know the difference?"

"But why?"

Cluff shrugged: "If she made Greensleeve believe that she wasn't alone, if he thought Carter was in it with her—"

"In what?"

"She'd a hold over him."

"The baby?"

"It could hardly have been the first money she'd got out of Greensleeve. He wouldn't be likely to pay any more willingly than the next man."

"She'd quarrelled with Carter."

"She wouldn't have shared with anybody. Only a fool would have thought she'd get support from Carter. She wasn't a fool. Carter was to let Greensleeve know she'd go to any lengths."

"It's only conjecture."

"Where else can we start?"

"We don't know he fathered it."

"It might have served its purpose just as well."

"If she followed him, to the Town Hall—"

"Motive. She was hounding him now. He couldn't know when she'd confront him in public. She meant him not to know. She let him see her behind him. He leaves his car at the back of the Town Hall when he's attending meetings. She could go out of the side door, into the car. It's dark there. He'd know that was what she'd done."

"He'd caught himself a tartar."

"He's never lived in Rupert Street."

"A man in his position—"

"Everyone's got a blind spot."

"He's married."

"Would he be less dictatorial at home than in public?"

"I'm sorry for his wife," Barker said.

Cluff warned him, "Don't turn into my kind of policeman. You won't be a success."

They climbed the hill, out of the town centre. Cluff added, after a few minutes, "Nothing's ever gone wrong for him. He's money, a reputation in local government, more than a voice—a say—in what goes on in Gunnarshaw. People dance when he calls the tune."

"Not you, Sergeant."

Cluff took this road every day, to and from his cottage two miles off. At one time the houses of the town had extended only halfway up the road, beyond that point fields. The fields had blossomed more lately, like a garden given over to weeds, into a rash of quickly-built semi-detached dwellings contrasting with the solider, more substantial detached houses nearer to the High Street. Space when these latter had been built wasn't at a premium. Their original owners, as anachronistic as the houses had become, had liked quiet and privacy. There weren't many of these mansions and they stood in grounds round which trees had grown into thick screens.

Cluff said, "Greensleeve knows what we think we know."

"Is that why you wouldn't let me bolt the gate of his yard last night?"

"Let him believe we know what we've still to find out. It might save us trouble in the long run."

They hadn't reached yet the modern erections of speculative builders. A short drive opened in a tall hedge growing high on a bank above a mortarless retaining wall. It curved between Scotch pines to the unseen door of a square house, rising at its corners into pseudo-turrets, a narrow branch diverging to a kitchen entrance at the back. Cluff said, "He must be proud to live here. His father and his grandfather had the rooms over the shop. He's come a long way. Money, not breeding's the yardstick of importance these days."

"He's done well for himself all right."

"What's left of the family that built this place hasn't got twopence to rub together."

A grass border edged the drive. Cluff stepped over it on to viscous soil under the trees. Windows at the side of the house overlooked the drive.

"I don't like this," Cluff said. "You go." He called Clive under the trees with him. He told Barker, "He even keeps a servant of sorts. Only an old woman. Some kind of relative." He added, "Try the back." Barker's feet crunched on the gravel. "Quietly," Cluff warned. "Leave his wife out of it if you can. You know what to ask."

"She can't be kept in the dark for ever."

"When I'm ready," Cluff said.

He leaned on his stick. Clive, catching his sense of melancholy, the melancholy of the dripping, overgrown garden, its dull shrubs, its dark trees, looked up at him, helpless to cheer him when he was in this mood. Neither the dog nor the man noticed a curtain flutter at one of the upstairs windows. Barker didn't come back.

The rain wept on him from the eyes of the trees. The winter afternoon waned to its close. He withdrew into himself, stifling thought, powerless to guide or control, too far on his way at this stage to go back, carried on by the tide of events. The sound of footsteps on the gravel penetrated his understanding but he didn't look up, waiting to hear Barker's voice. The footsteps stopped. He forgot them, sinking back into oblivion.

She said, "You don't have to hide from me."

He stepped over the verge again, on to the drive. He looked at Greensleeve's wife, trying to reconcile the tone of her voice with her appearance. Her words sounded cheerful, even triumphant, as if she welcomed his coming rather than feared it. She looked

weary and worn out, small like Greensleeve, both of them much
of a height, thin, her figure more masculine than feminine.

"Caleb Cluff," she said.

He remembered her, as he remembered all of his generation
still alive, in the dales round Gunnarshaw or in Gunnarshaw where
he had boarded on weekdays at the Grammar School. What he saw
both pleased him and depressed him. He could not recognize in
what Greensleeve had turned her into the girl Greensleeve had married. At the same time she justified both his pursuit of Greensleeve
and his growing certainty of Greensleeve's guilt. The pieces of the
puzzle that was no puzzle clicked farther into place, the reasons
for Greensleeve's defection more obvious. Observing her from
under lowered eyelids he could understand the impulse that had
compelled Greensleeve to place in jeopardy everything most dear
to him. Her fault or Greensleeve's wasn't important. The only fact
that mattered was the woman Cluff saw now.

It came to him more forcibly than ever that he could hardly
recall the time when he had last seen her in the town, years ago. She
had disappeared from general view at so distant a date in the past
that Gunnarshaw might well be forgiven for believing her already
dead. She seemed to him hardly alive as it was, ghastly, doll-like. His
heart lurched for the girl she had once been, a rung in the ladder
of Greensleeve's climb to urban glory, broken now, her purpose
served. She faced him, slovenly, careless, her hair awry, her stock-
ings wrinkled, not too clean. If anything of her youth had outlasted
her life with Greensleeve it was her eyes. Her eyes gazed at Cluff,
bright and sparkling. Her eyes were wrong, at odds with the rest
of her. He felt naked under them. They held more in them than a
girl's eyes held, something he could not interpret, beyond his grasp.

He stood quietly. They faced each other in the gloom of the sad garden. Her lips curled and she said, "Your man's in the kitchen." He could follow or not as he wished. He followed, his dog beside him.

Barker perched on the edge of a wooden chair, diffident, uneasy, embarrassed. The large room was intended not only for a kitchen but as living quarters for domestic staff. An old woman, older than Alice Greensleeve, not much neater but stouter, less defeated once and once surer of herself, watched Barker like a hawk. Cluff felt that the mistress had been the maid and the maid the mistress, but it didn't apply any more, the mistress in charge again and the maid confused and unbelieving.

"It's not a social call," Greensleeve's wife said. He knew that she mocked him, but he did not know why. It occurred to him that she would thank him if he freed her from her husband. She stared at him as if she was considering how he could be useful to her. He had more than a passing conviction that she regarded him as a tool. The positions they ought to have had were reversed, she the originator, himself the instrument.

They spoke their minds in the dales, without fear or favour. They said what they meant in the least possible number of words, without prevarication, refusing to evade the issue. He was a dales-man, with a reputation amongst dalesmen for directness, famous for his independence with men who called no man master. He sought for words and he couldn't find words. He began to get angry with himself and in the cold kitchen his cheeks warmed and went redder.

Her words were a statement of fact. "The murder," she said, the smile that was no smile playing on her lips, her eyes taunting. The brightness in her eyes was the brightness of fever not of youth.

He recognized it now if he had been deceived before. He looked down at his feet. What sort of game was this?

The servant, the dependent relative, whatever she was, frowned, transferring her attention from Barker to Greensleeve's wife, a jailer whose prisoner had been suddenly pardoned, lost at the abrogation of authority. Alice Greensleeve's eyes wandered to the old woman for a moment, challenging discipline, daring interference.

"We're involved in it," she told Cluff. "Of course we're involved in it. He'd be a fool who thought differently."

He couldn't bring himself to speak the usual empty excuses about a routine visit, for elimination rather than for information, that he might have uttered. She wouldn't have believed him. She looked into him and read his mind. If she was mildly surprised at his call it was only because he had delayed it for so long. He had an impression that she had been waiting for him.

He asked, "What time did your husband come in?" without apologies for bringing Greensleeve into it, not needing to elaborate the exact occasion he referred to. She showed no resentment at his question. It did not offend her in any way. She did not counter with a demand about why he asked it, how her husband was concerned. Indifference Cluff might have accepted, in view of her years with Greensleeve, the eagerness that bubbled in her stuck in his craw.

The old woman jerked like a marionette. Barker dropped his hat on the floor and stooped to retrieve it. Clive's hackles lifted.

"He was often late," Greensleeve's wife said. "He didn't spend much time at home."

She volunteered the information offhandedly and Cluff was certain that she knew what she was saying. The walls around him contracted, oppressive, and the atmosphere of the room hung about him like a material fog, heavy with long-standing hostility. He longed for the open air. The house was a house of adults, disillusioned, beyond dreams, lacking the presence of children, and the memory of children, with nothing to sweeten the disillusion of growing old, worse than the house in Rupert Street.

She asked, "What would Gunnarshaw do without him?" her voice level, her tone neutral, carefully avoiding the sarcasm and bitterness Cluff sensed nevertheless.

He thought back, trying to see her in those days more exactly, the daughter of a manufacturer, of little account in the world outside but big enough in Gunnarshaw, a self-made man fashioning a new Gunnarshaw, coloured by his own image. Whatever Greensleeve's views on the eligibility of a mistress the chemist had chosen a wife with an eye to the main chance, an only child with the inevitability of inheritance. She'd never attracted Cluff. He recalled her snobbish and spoilt, her nose in the air, holding her skirts against contact with more ordinary boys and girls.

She added, with the same air of impartiality, "And he's busy at the shop." She looked at Cluff archly. "Busy," she repeated, "with more than he can do by himself."

How did she know? Had she only suspected? Had Greensleeve, in a moment of lost self-control, mocked her with it, painting to her the picture of herself and comparing it with a picture of Jane Trundle? For some reason Cluff remembered Margaret in the shop, the bitterness and the contempt she directed at Greensleeve behind his back, the frustration of longing without gratification, the fear of surrender for which she never had opportunity. Margaret could have told Greensleeve's wife, Margaret active to snatch from others a prize she had no hope of gaining herself. It wasn't important. How

Alice Greensleeve knew was beside the point. She knew and she wouldn't admit she knew. Jane Trundle's death was no tragedy to her.

The old woman interrupted suddenly, "Not much after nine," and Barker jumped again. He looked anywhere but at Cluff. He cleared his throat nervously and prayed for Cluff to dismiss him.

It wasn't over yet. Alice Greensleeve remarked, imperturbably, "The clocks in this house are never right."

The old woman's tone grew shrill: "I heard him."

"She's old," Greensleeve's wife told Cluff, excusing the woman not blaming her.

Cluff had his watch in his hand, comparing it with a clock on the mantel. He said, "It's right now."

"I've my wits about me," the old woman screamed.

Alice Greensleeve continued, as though the servant hadn't spoken, "He hasn't been at home as early as that for years."

Cluff put his watch back.

"There's nothing to attract him here," Alice Greensleeve said, and moved to stand by the old woman's chair. She put a hand on the old woman's shoulder: "You shouldn't be up. You're not better."

"There's nothing wrong with me."

Greensleeve's wife turned to Cluff. "It's the time of the year. She's taken this way at the beginning of winter. She's been in bed for the last three days."

The old woman, her face contorted, asked thickly, "Where were you?"

"What a night," Alice Greensleeve said, "to go for a drive!"

They could have heard a pin drop in the silence that followed. Barker's mouth fell open. He gaped at Cluff. Cluff swayed a little on his feet, eyes almost shut.

"Where?" the old woman persisted. "Where? Where?"

"In bed too."

Cluff took a step towards the outer door.

"We're not young," Alice Greensleeve informed the room at large. "We've been married for a long time."

"Barker," Cluff said, backing to the door.

"There's nothing else to do. I go to bed before ten."

"You didn't see him," the old woman objected.

"We sleep in separate rooms," Alice Greensleeve remarked. "He doesn't disturb me when he comes in."

"Nine," the old woman muttered.

"Ten," Alice Greensleeve contradicted. "After ten. I don't sleep. I lie awake all night."

"Nine!"

"I hear everything." Her fingers tightened on the old woman's shoulder, gripping like a vice.

"Nine!" the old woman repeated.

"If you like," Alice Greensleeve agreed, glancing briefly at Cluff, dismissing the subject.

Barker wiped a film of sweat from his brow with the back of his hand. They could hear through the closed kitchen door the shrill voice of the old woman, arguing and protesting, the words indistinguishable. No one answered her. The sweat surprised Barker. He was colder than the afternoon warranted and not merely with the chill of the kitchen, which was little warmer than the garden.

Barker pulled his coat about him. He said, "I wouldn't care what happened to me so long as I didn't have to come home to that."

They turned right out of the drive, Barker following Cluff's lead, making up the hill not down it into Gunnarshaw. Clive ran ahead, relieved to be away from Greensleeve's. Barker's steps faltered. He thought he had been better off as a uniformed constable. He wondered where the glamour of crime had got to, the fights and adventures in the novels he read. He rubbed his hands together in a washing motion, as if a sordidness he had never imagined had dirtied him physically. Walking behind a silent Cluff a sympathy for Cluff welled up in him that he could not analyse. Cluff's back bent and Cluff did not hold himself as upright as he usually did. He made full use of his stick.

Barker quickened his pace. He came up with Cluff. He asked, "Are you going to the cottage?"

More loudly, Barker said, "Shall I go back to the station?"

Cluff halted. His head came round slowly. He gazed at Barker, amazed to see him. The Sergeant considered for a while, reaching for coherence. Completely unaware of either of Barker's questions he murmured, "I'm going home. There's nothing to do but wait."

Barker nodded. Cluff continued on his way. Clive looked up at Barker and went after Cluff. Barker hesitated, not knowing what was expected of him.

"Come with me," Cluff's voice came to his ears.

They passed the last of the houses, walking without speaking to each other. The road was familiar to Barker from yesterday morning. Yesterday morning was an eternity away. He remembered Inspector Mole's fulminations about Cluff's steadiness, the Inspector's irritation at Cluff's calm and apparent unconcern however important the event to Mole.

Barker wondered what the Inspector had to complain about. Barker tried to trace, step by step, the manner in which Cluff had collected his information, how Cluff had got to the point he'd reached. There was nothing connected, when Barker thought of it, in Cluff's meanderings here and there in Gunnarshaw, no hint of a prearranged plan of campaign. The thing seemed to grow of itself, round Cluff, without Cluff really having anything to do with it. Marching with the Sergeant, Barker was sure that the picture in Cluff's mind was sharper and more definite than the picture in his own. He felt a lessening of tension, a reduction of urgency. He found it quite natural that they were renouncing Gunnarshaw for the time being. What Cluff wanted to know would come to him of itself; he didn't have to go in search of it.

Rain blew in their faces, clean, refreshing, icy. Barker lowered his head against the force of the wind. They dropped, after the level stretch past the last of the houses, into a hollow where a stream, swollen with rain, gurgled through a culvert under the road, and climbed again, higher, more exposed to the weather. The fields lay sodden on either side of them, occupied only by a few bedraggled sheep hugging the shelter of walls and hedges. They didn't meet anybody on this minor road that led only to a succession of hamlets and farms. No traffic passed them either way. Cluff's step was firmer. He let the rain beat on him, meeting it four-square, refusing to bow to it.

Jenet had the cottage to herself when they reached it. The cat gave them no greeting, disdainful of their wet coats, wary of their approach to the fire Annie Croft had banked before she left.

"Let me help," Barker offered.

The constable, in the kitchen doorway, followed Cluff's movements in the kitchen. The Sergeant rooted in the cupboards for crockery and cutlery. He investigated the oven attached to its attendant cylinder of gas, discovering in it a meat and potato pie large enough to feed both Barker and himself three times over. A pantry overflowed with pastries, yellow buns, Eccles cakes, apples buried in crisp crusts, tarts smothered in jam. An army wouldn't go short here.

Gas hissed through the pipe from the cylinder. Cluff struck a match and lit the oven. He began to carry the crockery and the cutlery into the living-room. Barker brought a modicum of supplies from the pantry and Cluff sent him back sternly for more. The pie, beginning to get hot, filled the cottage with its savoury smell.

They sat back in their chairs, replete, Cluff's waistcoat unbuttoned, big mugs of tea by their empty plates as conclusion to their meal. Dark had fallen and the oil-lamp was lit, soft and amber, a perfect companion for the blazing fire. No sounds disturbed them except those they made themselves, easing in their seats.

Cluff reached for his mug. He sucked at its contents. He said over its rim to Barker, "Which of them did you believe?"

"Is there any doubt about it?" Barker sipped tea in his turn, the killing of Jane Trundle a long way off, something he didn't want to be bothered with just now, unreal and shadowy, not of any moment. He heard the gulp of liquid in Cluff's throat. The heat of the room and the contentment of his stomach made him sleepy. He murmured, with an effort, the servant at Greensleeve's house vague in his recollection, "She was old. She was ill. It's easy for her to have been mistaken."

"Or loyal," Cluff said. "Without Greensleeve who'll look after her, feed her, clothe her? Where will she find another roof to shelter under?" He got up from the table: "Bring your tea to the fire."

Jenet, ejected from Cluff's armchair, remembered her breeding and retained her dignity, expressing her annoyance only in the stiffness of her manner. She waited patiently for Cluff to settle himself, before jumping, as by right, on to his knees. He played with her ear and she shifted haughtily, coldly spurning an offer of peace.

"She's going to make sure," Cluff said.

They didn't need to elaborate. There was a connection between them, fostered by the cottage, a telepathy that allowed them almost to read each others' thoughts. Opposite to Cluff across the hearth Barker half-lay in his chair, his legs stretched out, Clive's head warm against an ankle. His hand gripped his mug, its broad bottom resting on the chair arm. The chair was deep and padded and big. He knew at once that Cluff meant the wife.

"She wants him arrested," Cluff added.

Barker allowed his thoughts to flow idly. He didn't consider them. He didn't grope for them. He wasn't sufficiently interested to interpret them. He had no feeling about them one way or the other. The implications of Cluff's remark floated in his mind. They knew already, he and Cluff, that Greensleeve had been farther that night than the streets of Gunnarshaw. The wife knew it too. Mud on Greensleeve's car, the unmade surface of the track through the plantation on the moor spattering the car. Beyond the plantation heather reaching with its tendrils to the very edge of the road, heather sapless at this time of year, its stalks brittle, disintegrating into little specks of vegetable matter mingling with the mud. Tiny remnants of moor growth washed from Greensleeve's car, stranded in the yard of Greensleeve's shop. Minute bits of matter in the infinitesimal cracks of Jane Trundle's shoes. Greensleeve going to his meeting, pursued by Jane Trundle. Greensleeve returning to his house at ten o'clock. The old woman lying, to protect her own future as much as Greensleeve's.

"Separate rooms," Cluff murmured.

Barker slid a little farther down in his chair. He was better off here. He didn't want to be anywhere else except here. What must life have been like in that big, old-fashioned house, grim in its grim, tree-choked garden, the trees cutting off light and air, weeping around it? They didn't sleep together. They went their own ways. Greensleeve went his own way: what way had Greensleeve's wife to go? Escaping upstairs at night, before he came in, to avoid him. Greensleeve seeking the sanctuary of his own room, no goodnight between them, no contact, each hating the sight of the other. The wife lying sleepless, waiting, listening, peeping from behind the curtains perhaps. His door closing. The minutes ticking away. The wife, holding herself in, controlling herself until it was safe, creeping soundlessly, prying, searching, not caring and still unable to rest, looking for what small indications he might have left in his wake of his evening's activities, twisting the knife in her wounds, feeding her hatred of him.

"A divorce would have finished him in his public life," Cluff said. "We're still puritans at heart in Gunnarshaw. Gunnarshaw's half a century behind the rest of the nation."

She couldn't get away from Greensleeve. He couldn't get away from her. He wasn't willing to pay the price. He wanted his cake and to eat it too. When had he failed before? The ease of a liaison with Jane Trundle, the pleasures his wife denied, of which she was incapable. His wife's money, the advantages of his connection with her family to start him years ago on his upward path. The balance-sheet of marriage, profit here, debit there. No divorce. A divorce not to be contemplated. Not by him. No scandal. Jane Trundle, perceptive, cold, reading him like a book, leading him on. Pay, and could he go on paying? A baby—

The eyes of the cat glared at Barker, narrow, green slits shading to yellow. Jenet watched him, suspicious of Barker's unfamiliarity, Barker an intruder in the cottage, unwanted, alien. Barker lifted himself higher in the chair, jerkily. Barker asked, "But would she have gone so far? What was the need of it? Was she so foolish as to believe there wasn't a breaking-point?" He meant Jane Trundle, not Greensleeve's wife.

"Anything within reason," Cluff said. "She must have known that. He'd have paid her anything in reason. She must have known. Would she have driven him to desperation?"

"Carter," Barker said, sitting up. "Could it have been Carter after all?"

"Not Carter."

Barker relaxed again. The room was too much for him, its quiet, its peace, its warmth. Let it be Greensleeve, then. He didn't care. You couldn't tell with people. He'd no business to be here, in this cottage. Cluff shouldn't be sitting over there. They were here and who was there to disturb them? Greensleeve or Carter, anyone else, the old woman in Greensleeve's house, Greensleeve's wife, Margaret at the shop or Jean, men in Gunnarshaw they didn't even know about. Greensleeve as good as anybody. Get it over with. Get it finished. Life waited. There were better ways of living.

"The hens," Cluff said. "I've forgotten to feed the hens."

Barker couldn't tell how it had come about. He was alone, Cluff in the cottage behind him. A hurricane lantern shed a warm glow on a sack of corn in a shed in the back garden. He didn't mind.

He looked forward all the more to the cottage again. He dug with his hands in the sack. The hard pellets of corn pattered like hail in the bottom of the bucket. Wind lashed his cheeks. The flame of the lantern flickered. His shoes sank in moist earth. He strained his eyes into the dark, the hen-hut looming. He wrestled with a wooden bar holding the door of the hut closed. He jumped back at the sudden flurry of movement, wings flapping, frightened hens flying amongst the perches, wakened, hysterical. He emptied his bucket on the floor and refastened the door.

Cluff hadn't stirred. The cat hadn't stirred on Cluff's lap. Clive lay in the same position on the rug. Barker, back in his chair, couldn't believe that he had moved either. He didn't think any more, not even unconsciously. What was there to think about?

Barker's hands gripped the arms of the chair. He crouched in the chair, ready to leap to his feet, tense with an unknown fear, ignorant of its cause. Clive had gone. Jenet, in Clive's place on the rug, licked a paw and washed her face fastidiously.

"Cluff," the Sergeant said in the passage, identifying himself.

"You!" Cluff said.

Barker held himself rigid, staring at the open door to the passage. Time stretched endlessly.

The cradle of the telephone tapped, oscillated by Cluff's fingers. "Hello? Hello?" Barker heard. "Are you still there? Hello?"

Cluff in the doorway, hat askew on his head, arms tangled in the sleeves of his Burberry. Cluff saying, "Get the car."

"The car?"

"Quickly."

Barker couldn't remember seeing the car anywhere except on the setts in the High Street where he had parked it yesterday when he had driven himself in from the cottage in search of Cluff. He knew Cluff must have walked back last night after they had been to the yard behind Greensleeve's shop. Cluff had walked into Gunnarshaw again this morning.

"It's not here," Barker said.

# CHAPTER IX

GREENSLEEVE, IN THE DOORWAY OF HIS SHOP, WATCHED Cluff round the corner by the church. He saw only Cluff, not Barker by Cluff's side nor Clive at Cluff's heels. His hair was wet with rain, his neat suit damp with rain. He felt Margaret's eyes on him, boring into his back.

He couldn't see Cluff any longer. Across the High Street rain danced on the steps of the Town Hall. Rain blackened its smooth stone pillars. The finger of its flagpole on the roof stabbed accusingly at the low, dark clouds.

His gaze wandered up the High Street, down the High Street, his preserve for as long as he could remember, taking in its shops and banks and offices, its hotels, its old buildings interspersed with newer, taller buildings, flashier and more vulgar. It belonged to him, from the moment of his birth in the room above the shop. It was a part of him, the frame in which he lived and breathed, his kingdom, the extent and compass of his rule. The injustice of his case weighed on him intolerably. He felt, for the first time in his life, the fates against him. He was trapped, unfairly, rejected, without warning, by Gunnarshaw, this the end of his efforts for Gunnarshaw, this the thanks of its people, the reward they offered him. He couldn't understand how the relief of yesterday had turned so suddenly into the hopelessness of today, the Indian summer of his escape from Jane Trundle into the winter of his unmerited overthrow.

He saw the High Street with new eyes, not his realm but Cluff's. Contemptuous of Cluff's ability, he hated Cluff and he was afraid of Cluff, Cluff Gunnarshaw not himself, Cluff the moors about Gunnarshaw, Gunnarshaw Cluff's ally not his, banding itself with Cluff against him. Gunnarshaw wasn't Greensleeve, go-ahead, modern, properly appreciative of the age in which it existed. Gunnarshaw had deceived him, smiling on him only to withdraw its favour. The town was Cluff, sprawling, untidy, rooted to the soil from which it sprang, akin to the hills that sheltered it, wild and unchanged from the beginning of time. Gunnarshaw drowned in the mire of its own obstructive tradition. It clung leech-like to the past, spurning the progress that Greensleeve promised. Where else but in Gunnarshaw would he have stood condemned, driven to his ruin for so little a sin? Where else a Cluff, in these modern days, to hunt the spirit rather than the fact of a crime?

The man at the fruit-stall, Cluff's friend, Cluff's vantage-point, lounged behind the curtain of rain streaming from the tarpaulin that served him as roof. Even from this distance Greensleeve could not mistake the suspicions slowly developing in the man's mind, peeping through the windows of his eyes in the chemist's direction. The man's wife was with him, farther back under the awning, but looking where her husband looked. Cluff's friends, or Cluff's spies?

The watchers he had imagined a short time ago, when he stood with Cluff in the rain, again obsessed Greensleeve. He was the object not of two pairs of eyes but of a hundred pairs of eyes. The windows on the other side of the street, the doorways to right and left of the one he stood in, were more than ever the refuge of his concealed enemies. Faces hid themselves behind the stacked tins and the pyramided packets in the grocer's, between the suits and shirts in the windows of an outfitter's. They showed briefly in the gaps of a barrier of shoes and boots ranged in serried ranks in a shop selling footwear. The owners of offices and their clerks dodged on upper storeys, camouflaged by the painted letters on the glass through which they looked, spelling out the names of themselves and the nature of their businesses.

He shuddered, cringing under their speculation, convinced that it was real. He could believe that they were surprised to see him, coatless, without a hat, wet, for once neither brash nor busy nor supercilious. He could not believe that they were sorry for him. He had no confidence in the protestations with which they had greeted him in the past. If they had been his friends their affection was meaningless, their friendliness a myth. They were on Cluff's side now, himself betrayed, glad to see him defeated.

His spirit sank. The street had never been so empty and deserted, his customers so few as this afternoon. They joined against him even in advance of Cluff.

He fled for the shelter of his shop, to be welcomed only by Margaret's sneering grin. He looked about for Jean, and he remembered. He remembered Jean hurrying away from him in the street. That Margaret still remained filled him with astonishment.

He sat behind his desk in his dispensary, what little courage he retained seeping away because of Jean. Cluff with Jean in the street outside the shop yesterday morning, Cluff with Jean again while Greensleeve lunched, confident and assertive, in false security. Jean a third time, going where? After Cluff, if she hadn't come face to face with her employer, to tell Cluff at last what she knew.

He tried to pull himself together, the victim of his own cowardice. He had nothing to fear, nothing that the law could punish him for. He thought that, of the two alternatives, the punishment of the law would be preferable, less severe, more merciful, than

the never-ending punishment of Gunnarshaw. He could not forget
Cluff. What was Cluff interested in? What mystery was there about
murder in a town like Gunnarshaw? He couldn't forget Jean. Jean
and Cluff. Any policeman in the country but Cluff would have
had the case finished in a day, Carter safely under lock and key,
the evidence marshalled in the unlikely event of Carter failing to
confess. They'd known it, all of them, everyone in Gunnarshaw.
They'd been certain, as Greensleeve was certain, of Carter's guilt.
Only Cluff stood out and they followed Cluff like sheep a shepherd,
veering to Cluff's lead, weather-cocks at the mercy of every breeze.

Could he abdicate so easily? Was it inescapable even yet? He
passed Margaret in the shop, ignoring her, as if she wasn't there.
He wore his hat and his coat this time. He stared at Gunnarshaw,
brought to a halt on the pavement by Gunnarshaw's contrariness.
Traffic flowed in the roadway. People passed him. He couldn't
distinguish, from what he saw, between this afternoon and any
other. Even the man at the fruit-stall had his back turned, filling a
brown-paper bag with apples for a woman engaged in conversation
with the stall-holder's wife. For a heart-leaping moment Greensleeve
thought the girl coming towards him was Jean, a chit of a girl, a
third of his age.

A voice addressed him by name. He took a grip on himself and
turned to Inspector Mole, in his dark-blue, belted coat and his flat
police cap, the silver of his rank on his shoulders. Mole smiled, suit-
ably humble, respectful as always. If Mole didn't know, why should
anyone know? Wasn't there a chance still? His sins, Greensleeve
told himself, didn't include the ultimate sin. How could he rely
on his own assessment of the actions of the unpredictable Cluff?
Who knew, with Cluff, what the man was thinking, whether he

had facts to support his blundering, or no facts at all? The man was a charlatan, a *poseur*, acting the part he happened to look, the bluff countryman, the man of the dales. Inside there was nothing, no ability, no brain, only an emptiness he spent his days trying to conceal.

"I'm looking for the Sergeant," Mole said pleasantly.

"The Sergeant," Greensleeve repeated, the tone of his words striking an answering spark from Mole.

"You've not seen him by any chance?" Mole asked, clearly expecting a negative reply.

"He was here," Greensleeve said, recalling that he was Greensleeve, with authority in Gunnarshaw and the power of position over men like Mole and Cluff. He added, boldly, "He's been here for most of the day. He was here yesterday. No doubt he'll be here again tomorrow."

"Always to be found," Mole said, "except when he's wanted."

"I think sometimes," Greensleeve told the Inspector, "the High Street's his natural environment. He gives me the impression that he grows in the High Street, that he's stood in the High Street for so long he's struck roots."

Mole's features moved expressively, agreeing with the chemist, indicating his inability to keep Cluff in order and his resentment because of it. His manner asked, as intelligibly as if he had said it, "What can you do with a man like that?"

"It's a small town," Greensleeve remarked.

"You're right, Mr. Greensleeve."

"We've been expecting an arrest."

Mole shrugged.

"That's his car," the chemist said and Mole scowled at the car, its age and its dilapidation an insult to the uniform he wore.

"Come in for a while," the chemist invited.

"You're going out."

"It's not important. If you want Cluff this is the place to wait for him."

Mole said, "You wouldn't think Gunnarshaw had a police-station, would you?"

The Inspector put his cap on Greensleeve's desk. He said, man-to-man, to Greensleeve sitting across from him, "It's not a nice thing to be involved in, even so remotely as you are."

"I'd help if I could," Greensleeve said. "The Sergeant's methods are his own." He waited and Mole kept silent. "He's had his successes," the chemist added.

"One," Mole corrected, morosely. "A chance in a million."

"He's grown up in these parts."

"He doesn't let us forget it." Mole implied that if Cluff's birth was any advantage it wasn't to the police.

Greensleeve drummed on the desk with his fingers: "You haven't heard anything from Superintendent Patterson?"

"Not me."

"I've been in touch with him," Greensleeve admitted.

"It might help," Mole replied, misunderstanding the chemist.

"I gather Cluff's well thought of at Headquarters."

Mole turned on his seat. The dispensary door was open. He could see through the shop and the glass panel of the shop door, into the High Street. "I'm wasting your time," he said.

Greensleeve motioned him back into the chair: "The town's full of rumour."

"I've always said, there's no smoke without fire."

"The Sergeant doesn't think so, evidently."

Mole's scowl spread farther over his face.

"I shouldn't ask—" Greensleeve began.

"In your position, Mr. Greensleeve—" Mole protested.

"He's seen Carter, of course."

Mole nodded.

"But not detained him?"

Mole made a motion of denial.

"No doubt the Sergeant knows what he's doing," Greensleeve tried. "Perhaps, at least, Carter helped?"

"Not that I'm aware of."

"Surely—The boy knew her well."

"He's not saying anything."

"Indeed?"

Mole looked at the chemist, taken aback by his eager tone.

Greensleeve added quickly, "It's not good for the town—"

Mole said, subsiding, "Between ourselves, the boy's neither alibi nor excuse."

"Alibi?"

"We know approximately when she died." He had Greensleeve's interest. "After nine," he continued. "Nearer to ten o'clock," determined to consolidate himself with a man of influence.

"You won't be arresting me then," Greensleeve smiled. "I was at home by that time."

Mole looked shocked, as if the joke was in bad taste. He said, "Really, Mr. Greensleeve—" indicating his belief that the heavens would fall before any such eventuality occurred.

"Perhaps I shouldn't tell you," Mole said. He hesitated, so that Greensleeve shouldn't underestimate the value of his revelation. "But you won't pass it on. She was pregnant."

It was Greensleeve's turn to look shocked: "You astonish me."

"You can't tell what they're like these days," Mole said. "Even the best of them." He paused. "I've two daughters of my own."

Greensleeve said, "The father?"

"There's only one candidate for my money."

"Carter?"

"We haven't heard of anyone else she was mixed up with."

"Can't Carter—?"

Mole succeeded this time in getting to his feet without interruption.

Greensleeve elaborated, "Wasn't he likely to have known? He wouldn't let her alone. If there'd been anyone else—"

"I don't think so."

Greensleeve came round the desk: "You won't wait for the Sergeant?"

"I'll go back to the station."

"Is there any message I can—?"

Mole said, "We can't expect you to do our work for us, Mr. Greensleeve."

Greensleeve, still in his hat and coat, went with him into the shop. Mole looked hard at Margaret, who returned his look without flinching. The Inspector opened his mouth and thought better of the question he had been going to ask. In the street, where Margaret couldn't hear them, he told Greensleeve, "I wondered for a moment if she knew anything."

"Wouldn't she have come to me? Besides, she's had plenty of opportunity. The Sergeant's been so prominent I almost began to believe he had us under special observation."

"Your other assistant—"

"Jean?"

"That's why I'm looking for Cluff. She came to the station a short time ago."

"Jean did?"

"Oughtn't she to be at work?"

"Hardly. How shall I put it—that we've severed our association?"

"Sacked?"

"She's never been reliable. Whatever it is she wants, I'd be inclined not to accept at its face value—"

"I don't know what she wants," Mole said angrily. "She refused to talk to me. It had to be Sergeant Cluff or nothing." He mimicked Jean's voice.

"She's still there?"

"She wouldn't wait either."

The clock in the church tower struck a quarter. "If you'll excuse me," Greensleeve said, pretending that the chime had jogged his memory.

"I shouldn't have kept you," Mole apologized, uncertain whether or not Greensleeve heard him.

Greensleeve banged the door of his car shut. He had some difficulty in finding his engine key and his hand trembled as he inserted it. Gears scraped and the engine stalled. He didn't look up at Mole, on the pavement. The engine fired and the car backed, with a jerk, into the carriageway. Mole wagged his head in deprecation.

He had no real notion which direction to take. He wrenched the wheel, intent on getting out of Mole's sight, tense with an urgency he did not know how to satisfy. Carter knew nothing. Jane had told Carter nothing. Cluff had nothing to go on except the mutual dislike he and Greensleeve had for one another, men by temperament at opposite poles, completely irreconcilable.

Somewhere from the dregs of memory Greensleeve dredged a recollection of Jean's address. He swerved left and, after some distance, right, into the part of Gunnarshaw known, from the names of the streets, as Little Crimea, built after the war of the mid-eighteen-fifties.

He forced himself to dawdle along Sevastopol Road, watching the pavements, praying for a glimpse of Jean. A little group of women, with prams and dogs on leads, congregated round the gates of a primary school waiting for their elder offspring, sheltering under umbrellas. Past the school he saw no one except a woman or so, hurrying home from shopping, too shapeless and broad to attract his attention for more than an instant.

In the growing dark, with the gas-lamps not yet lit, he had difficulty in identifying his whereabouts, this section of the town unfamiliar to him except on paper in his capacity as councillor. Narrower streets branched off on both sides of the car, those on his right rising slightly, the ones on his left climbing steeply, but all unmade, muddy in the rain apart from the flagged sidewalks, weed-filled and stony. He strained for the letters on the white plates, fixed halfway up the corner houses. He almost missed Balaclava Street and he had to reverse in order to see up its length. He sat in the car. Some of the women he had passed earlier at the school straggled by, with the full tally of their children.

He felt naked in spite of the deserted road, the centre of an unseen scrutiny as he had been in the High Street, the carefully draped net over the windows here even better concealment for observers than the goods on show in the shops, giving watchers a clear field of vision, hiding them from him entirely. He could not delude himself, in any case, that his car would go unrecognized in a place where it had no right to be, or that his presence would not be reported in due course to Cluff.

He continued to wait, alternating between hope and fear, wondering whether it would be worth his while if he offered to withdraw the complaint about Cluff he had made to Patterson. The lamps on the kerbs lit up and he had to switch on his own lights. The windows of the houses about him, at their fronts, stayed dark.

His resolution broke. He crawled in low gear farther along Sevastopol Road, to its junction with another road. He went round the corner, his windscreen wipers scraping softly. Pools of dark lay in the road between the gas-lamps, the blacker for the glow of the lamps islanded in the night. His sidelights didn't serve. The beams of his headlights cleft the darkness in front of him, putting the gas-lamps to shame.

He stamped on the brake. The steering-wheel hit him painfully in the chest. His head almost crashed against the windscreen as he was thrown forward. He caught at his breath, his eyes unbelieving. He couldn't credit what he saw.

Carter came from the door of a cheap café. The lights in the windows of the café went out, while Carter waited. A short, dumpy girl pulled the door to and bent to lock it. She joined Carter, putting an arm through Carter's arm. They started to cross the road. Greensleeve rubbed his eyes. The light of a gas-lamp fell on them and he must be mistaken. They came into the path of his own headlights, cautiously, looking towards him, not quite sure that the car had really stopped, giving them time to get over. The car stood in the middle of the road, equidistant from either pavement.

They were hurrying now. Greensleeve worked the handle of his window frantically. He stuck his head out. He shouted, "Carter! Carter!" The couple stopped dead in their tracks.

"Why don't you confess?" Greensleeve yelled. "You know you killed her. Why don't you confess?"

The girl was pulling at Carter, trying to drag him away. In Greensleeve's headlights the sap seemed to go out of Carter. He started to crumple, bonelessly, and the girl held him. Her mouth worked, encouraging or consoling him. He abandoned himself to her, stumbling blindly at her direction. She tugged harder, trying to increase their speed.

"They won't hang you," Greensleeve shouted. "It wasn't your fault."

They began to run, both Carter and the girl, out of the glare.

Greensleeve's voice, high-pitched, screamed, "You've got to tell. You don't want innocent people to suffer, do you? Clear your conscience. Find Cluff. Tell Cluff you killed her. Tell him! Tell him!"

He couldn't see them. He couldn't hear them. They'd gone. He was trembling in the driving-seat, unable to control his body. He scrabbled at the knot of his tie, pulling his collar open, gasping for breath. Doors on to the pavements had begun to open. People looked out, calling to each other from house to house, pointing.

He got the engine going. Somehow he turned his car in the road, going back the way he had come. He couldn't go straight on. The road sloped upwards, coming to a dead end, blocked by a barrier of iron railings fencing off a recreation ground. The line of buildings on one side of him, except for the narrow gaps of footways, stretched continuous. He'd no option. He had to drive into Sevastopol Road again.

His brain whirled. Time meant nothing to him. He couldn't remember how long it was since Jean had fled from him in the High Street. He had to find her. He had to get to her before Cluff did.

He wasn't stopped opposite the end of Balaclava Street, but a little farther down Sevastopol Road. The yards behind the even-numbered houses in Balaclava Street faced the backyards of the houses on one side of its neighbour, a paved track just wide enough for a coal-lorry between their respective walls.

His heart fluttered and began to pound. His throat dried. He attempted to swallow and couldn't. The back street on which his eyes were glued had only a single lamp in the whole of its length. The lamp was more than enough. He couldn't mistake the figure turning out of one of the yards, walking insolently down the slope.

His hand clutched the handle of the car door. The door swung partly open. He had one foot on the road. He was half-in and half-out of the car, stuck there, unable either to retreat or to advance, wanting to shout, to yell, the words piling in his gullet.

Tall, her heels tapped on the pavement in Sevastopol Road. She couldn't miss seeing the car on the far side of the road, opposite the end of the back street. She ignored the car, carrying herself proudly.

Greensleeve sank back. Her hate of him was purposeless, irrational.

The shop at the corner of one of the side-streets along the road doubled as a sub-post office. A telephone kiosk reared beside the closed shop door. The light in the kiosk shone brightly through its glass panels. He could see her in the kiosk, in the light, bathed in the light, fully visible to her waist. She riffled the pages of a directory. She lifted the receiver. She had coins in one hand, a finger of the other hand ready on the dial. She held the receiver to her face.

Her lips moved. While she talked she stared out of the kiosk, at the car. A man Greensleeve had never seen before appeared from nowhere. He walked to the telephone kiosk and stood where the light of the kiosk fell on him. He waited his turn, impatient.

Margaret saw the car go past. She said into the telephone, "But I've just been to her home in Balaclava Street. She hasn't been back since she left the shop."

Margaret listened.

Margaret went on, "She'd something to tell you. The Inspector came to the shop this afternoon, looking for you. She'd been to the police-station. You weren't there."

Margaret replaced the receiver. She came out of the kiosk and the man outside brushed past her and shut himself in. Margaret stayed on the pavement, in the light, close to the kiosk, making quite certain that the road was empty. She lived in Sevastopol Road, only a few doors away.

# CHAPTER X

GREENSLEEVE'S FOOT PRESSED HARD ON THE ACCELERATOR. He roared up the High Street, past the church. He couldn't think of any other way to take.

His speed increased, his own garden on one side of him, the house where he lived, in which his wife was always waiting for him. He wasn't thinking of his house or of his wife. He had no intention of stopping.

A figure leapt into the road, from the entrance to his drive, waving its arms, long skirt flapping round its calves, a shawl slipping from its shoulders, muffled and wrapped like a mummy. He recognized it just in time.

The car lurched. Its tail swung, grazing the stone wall, metal screeching. The face at the window by his side grimaced. He mumbled, weak with shock. He could hear a spate of words, making no sense. After a while he recovered sufficiently to say, "I nearly killed you—"

She didn't listen to him. The violence of the explanation he hadn't taken in set her coughing. A paroxysm of coughing convulsed her. She held to the car, bent double, fighting to regain her breath.

She gasped, choking, "Cluff was here. I've been trying to get you at the shop. Cluff was asking about you. Cluff wanted to know where you were on the night of the murder."

He opened his mouth to protest, refusing to believe her.

"She lied," the old woman managed. "She lied deliberately. I've been waiting here in the rain. I'm not fit to be out. I've caught my death."

"Lied?" he said, mystified.

"It wasn't after ten," the woman said. "It wasn't much after nine. I heard you. I heard the car."

He stiffened, rigid, sweat breaking out on his forehead.

"Cluff believed it. Cluff wouldn't listen to me," the old woman sobbed. "What are they trying to do to you?"

The car rocked, its rear bumper caught in a crevice in the wall. The offside back wheel, where the car was on the wrong side of the road, spun in the cavity of a drain, polishing the bars of its grating. Another car drew up behind him. Greensleeve thought a voice asked, "Are you in trouble?"

He let the car take charge. Metal protested shrilly. Metal buckled and rent. The tyres gripped. He leapt forward with a jolt, trying to control his sudden freedom. Lights coming down the hill dazzled him. He flung an arm across his eyes. Somebody screamed.

Up the hill, racing, on to the level road at the top, down the incline to the hollow. No houses now. No lights except the dancing twin beams of his headlights. Cluff sneaking into the shop. Cluff sneaking into his house. Cluff badgering his assistants. Cluff putting lies into his wife's mouth. Cluff's spies everywhere. Cluff weaving a shroud to fold him in. Cluff a spider in the middle of his web, watchful, inexorably patient, calm, waiting for Jean. Why? Why? Why?

Wind whistled past Greensleeve's ears. Rain drenched him through the window he had neglected to close.

The girl ran like a rabbit in his headlights, frantic, from this side of the road to that. She gained the grass verge. She jumped the ditch awkwardly. She was too big for the hedge. The hedge was too thick for her to break through.

He was running himself, the door of his car swinging in the wind, the lights of the car blazing, the car in the middle of the road behind him. He knew he was shouting. She'd abandoned her attempt to penetrate the hedge. She stumbled in the shadow of the hedge, head down, shoulders bent, arms pressed close to her sides. If his pleas carried to her above the noise of the night, the thumping of her blood in her ears, she paid no attention to his pleas. His heart swelled to bursting. He realized too late that he should never have left the car, that he should have driven past her and come back down the hill to meet her. Too late for that. Too late now. He could make out, as she could, a gap in the hedge, the vague outline of a gate into the pasture behind the hedge. The night was dark, no moon or stars. Once out of the range of his headlights, in the blackness of the fields, he'd lose her. He couldn't keep this up. The distance between them was increasing already. If her fear equalled his, fear lending wings to them both, she had the advantage of him in years.

The edge of the ditch crumbled. She staggered, clutching the empty air. He called on his last resources, his panting mingling with hers. She toppled forward on to her face, evading in her fall his outstretched hands. He had a dim impression of her squirming and twisting and he was collapsing too, on top of her, into her warm softness.

He lay there. He couldn't get up. Someone was talking, begging. Someone was screaming. The words might have been his, the screams hers. He couldn't tell.

The words went on. The screams stopped. She quietened beneath him. His hands caressed rounded, smooth flesh. He could feel a pulse beating in her throat. They lay there eternally, time relative, all silence now, each moment a lifetime, bodies pressed together, throbbing, all other motion stopped, each of them waiting.

He moved first, rolling away. He struggled to his hands and knees, his chest heaving, his head lolling. He didn't know where the sounds were coming from. He'd no breath left. She wasn't making these noises.

The road cut a line across the sky, at the top of the hill, blacker below, less black above. Black shapes breasted the crest, outlined, shrinking from the feet up. Weary beyond measure he hauled himself upright. He stared down at the inert girl, sorry for her, sorry for himself. He could hear a dog barking.

He ran again. He had to run, in the shelter of the hedge as she had run, but downhill, in the direction of his car, trying to keep out of the track of its lights. The dog at his heels spurred him on. The skin of his back crawled in anticipation of the dog's teeth. He could hear, "Clive! Clive!"

A wave of dark engulfed him, past the car. He'd no time to jump for the car, no time to start its engine, no time to avoid with the help of the car the shouting men pounding after him. He swerved, with the inspiration of despair, behind the car, across the road. By a miracle the hedge on that side thinned. A short stretch of fencing blocked his way. He could make out the rails of the fence broken, sagging from its posts. He flung himself into the muddy grass, worming under the rails.

Barker, blinded by the sudden transition from light to dark, chased on down the road. The dog had passed as well, too excited to note how his quarry had doubled.

Greensleeve, hidden, silent in the fields, went on drunkenly. He splashed through a stream. The legs of his trousers clung to his calves. Water squelched in his shoes at each tottering step he took. Sometimes he slowed almost to a stop. Sometimes he trotted a few stumbling paces before his palpitating, aching limbs forced him to slow again. His head seemed about to explode. He couldn't see the ground. He pushed through hedges that barred his way or climbed clumsily over walls, barking his shins, skinning his hands, bringing top-stones down in his wake. He didn't know where he was going. He didn't know what he'd done. He couldn't think of anything except Jean underneath him, Jean still, and his fingers tensing.

Cluff, on one knee, lifted her in his arms. Barker's feet rattled on the road against the background of Clive's barks.

His hands touched her gently, groping for signs of life. Her head rolled and he pressed her closer in his arms to steady her. She stirred briefly. He propped her against his thigh and struggled out of his Burberry, wrapping her in it. He stayed very still, not moving.

He heard feet ringing again on the metalled road, slowly, with a heavy, hopeless tread. He looked up. He felt the nudging of Clive's muzzle. Barker, conquered, appeared in the light from the car.

Barker said, "I lost him. I went as far as the first houses. He wasn't anywhere to be seen."

Rain slanted in the beams of the headlights. Rain fountained on the shiny, black road.

"It's Greensleeve's car," Barker said.

She moved a second time. Her eyes stared up into his face, the lids fluttering over them. Her lips compressed and parted. He bent his head closer to her, his ear near her mouth, striving to hear her whispers. She fought against him, her strength returning, and he restrained her, quietening her fear little by little.

"He's gone," Cluff said. "You're safe now."

Her writhing stopped. She lay back, letting her body sag. He
gained his feet without letting her go and supported her to the car.

"How—?" she began.

"Margaret," Cluff said.

"I was coming to you. I couldn't find you in the town. I waited
and waited—"

"I'll take you home."

"I didn't dare go home till I'd found you. My parents—I walked
out of the shop."

"Don't worry about it."

She straightened in the seat by the driving-wheel. She put out a
hand and got hold of Cluff's sleeve, where he was standing in the
road by the open door. "I saw them," she said.

"Greensleeve and Jane Trundle?"

"One evening when I went back. I'd forgotten—my compact, a
glove, I can't remember—in the cloakroom behind the dispensary.
I knew he was still there, that she was with him. I didn't think. I
knocked at the dispensary door. The shop was dark, only a line of
light under the door into the dispensary. It didn't occur to me. I
opened the door—" She covered her face with her hands.

Barker's feet scraped on the road.

"What will happen to him?" the girl asked, and Cluff sighed.

"I couldn't believe that he'd killed her," Jean said.

Neither Barker nor Cluff contradicted her.

"I wasn't sure," Jean added. "I thought sometimes I must have
dreamed it."

"It was real," Cluff said.

"He never mentioned it. I told no one except Margaret."

"It doesn't matter."

Jean asked in a low voice, not looking at the Sergeant, "She was his mistress?" She read the answer in Cluff's face. She said, "I tried to think it hadn't anything to do with her murder. I couldn't decide. If it hadn't and I'd told—If people in Gunnarshaw got to know."

"He was more afraid of that than of anything."

Cluff nodded to Barker. Barker walked round the car to the driving-seat.

Jean murmured, "He began to talk about Jack Carter. Everyone was talking about Carter. Margaret said—I had to tell you then."

Cluff got into the back of the car. He called Clive in after him. Barker turned the car in the gateway Jean had never been able to reach in her flight from Greensleeve. They drove back along the road towards Gunnarshaw.

"Stop!" Cluff ordered.

He stood beside the car, halted up the hill a couple of hundred yards from Greensleeve's drive. Barker switched off the engine. Cluff shook his head. He said, "Take Jean home."

Barker started to object.

"She's had enough for one night," Cluff said.

"You'll wait for me to come back?" Barker pressed him anxiously.

"He might not be in there."

"Where else?"

Cluff was already moving down the road in front of the car. Barker reached back for the rear door Cluff had shut behind him. He opened the door and let Clive out.

When the car drove past Cluff, picking up speed, man and dog were walking together.

# CHAPTER XI

H E CAME FROM THE FIELDS, INTO THE GARDEN ON THE SIDE of the house away from the road. The old woman at the table in the kitchen, her arms on the table, her head lying on her arms, roused herself and looked up. He saw the horror in her face as she gazed at him. She pulled herself to her feet, holding to the table, her mouth gaping, her eyes wide.

He ignored the old woman, aware of her and yet not aware of her, as familiar to him as a piece of furniture. He crossed the kitchen, making for the door in its opposite wall. He was surprised to find the old woman in front of him, her arms outstretched. This additional obstacle irritated him, goading him beyond endurance.

Her lips moved. He could see her toothless gums. Her thin grey hair hung in wisps over her eyes. She wouldn't get out of his way. "No," the old woman said. "No."

Greensleeve couldn't follow. He wrenched at her arms. He tore her arms away. "Go to Cluff," the old woman was begging. "Tell Cluff everything. It's your only chance."

She clung to him, fighting him. "Cluff," she breathed. "Cluff! Don't you see yet?"

He disentangled himself again from her grip. She wouldn't leave him alone. She wouldn't understand. As often as he pushed her away she returned to the attack, hindering him, wasting his precious time, her words more incoherent, less and less intelligible. He thought he heard, "That devil!" but he wasn't paying attention, his mind elsewhere. "That devil! That devil!" she repeated, her voice seeming to come from very far away.

He didn't think. He brushed her aside. She tottered, off balance, and clutched at a chair. He clenched his fist and hit her as hard as he could, his blow falling on her neck. He continued to the door from which she had separated him, relieved to be rid of her. He didn't notice that her fingers let go of the chair, that she slid to the floor and lay still.

His wife, her hands in her lap, sat quietly in the sitting-room. She stared into space with an expression half vacant, half cunning, her mind planning, mapping the progress of her plot, the room dark, unlit, no fire burning in the grate. Little by little she grew conscious of the disturbance in the kitchen. She smiled to herself. She moved slowly, into a wide hall, feeling for a light-switch. She depressed the switch. A low-powered bulb came on, lighting the hall dimly.

Stairs mounted to the upper storey, broad, like the hall thickly carpeted. By the side of the stairs, between them and the wall, a passage led back to the kitchen.

She strolled nonchalantly, over the floor of the hall to where the passage began. She put a hand on the newel post, standing at the bottom of the stairs, leaning comfortably, perfectly at ease. Her husband swayed at the end of the passage, framed in the kitchen doorway.

She watched him, calmly, making no effort to go to him. Her eyes glinted but her face gave away nothing of the exultation she felt boiling inside her.

He bore no resemblance to the neat, well-brushed, well-groomed Greensleeve who had left that morning, as every morning, without a word of farewell. His hand on the wall smeared the wallpaper with a brown patch. He had lost his hat and the rain had plastered his hair to his skull, matting it down on his forehead, revealing more clearly the expanding baldness on his crown he so carefully trained his hair to conceal. His coat, disreputable and earth-stained, hung open, one of its buttons and the cloth where the button had been sewn torn off. A second button dangled from a thread, swinging to the motion of his body. His trousers were caked with mud. Mud covered his sodden, disintegrating shoes. Rents split his clothing where rusty nails in the fences he had climbed had snatched at it. His face was smudged. His hands were bleeding. He was filthy, daubed with dirt from head to feet. He looked at her with an expression she had never seen before, admitting his defeat, surrendering to her.

She prayed for his legs to fail him. She wanted fiercely to see him crawling to her on his hands and knees, reaching for her legs, bending his head to kiss her feet. She read her name in the silent movement of his lips, his plea for help.

He let go of the wall. He drove himself forward, stumbling, hardly able to keep himself up. She let him come. His eyes fixed on her, unwinking, drawing from her strength to continue. She had only to put out a hand and she could have touched him.

She stared back at him. Intentionally, spurning him, she half-turned. She started to go up the stairs. He grabbed at the newel post to save himself. He rotated round it and lay stretched on the bottom steps of the flight of stairs. "I didn't kill her," he was muttering.

She walked, giving him time to follow, along the landing, past the doors on either side of her, to the door of her own room at the far end of the landing. She opened the door and turned to face him. "No," she said, "You killed me."

She went to him. She dragged and pulled him into the bedroom. Inside she thrust him suddenly away. He fell backwards against the open door, his weight pushing it closed. He went with it, leaning against it, breathing heavily, resting, waiting until he recovered something of his strength.

She eyed him from the middle of the room, by her bed. "I knew," she told him, with a scorn that crushed him. "Did you imagine you could keep it from Cluff?" Only the door at his back kept him on his feet.

"Forgive me," he managed at last.

She laughed: "Will Gunnarshaw forgive you? Will Gunnarshaw forget?"

He sobbed, "I couldn't bear it—"

"Everything gone," she taunted. "For her! Your fine importance. Your cherished position. Your dignity. Your reputation. The respect they had for you."

"Is it too late?"

"The idol overturned. The mighty fallen—"

He said, wonderingly, "But I didn't kill her," repeating his denial.

"Who will believe you?"

"It's true," he insisted.

"Where have you been? What have you been doing?"

"I've tried," he said. "To keep Gunnarshaw from knowing. It's all I'm guilty of."

"Did you think at first you were free? Did you believe you were safe at last when you heard of her death?"

He couldn't argue with her.

"I'm glad," she said.

"I paid," he replied. "I'd have gone on paying—"

She said, "It's better than I'd hoped for. You've played into my hands, into Cluff's hands. You've put the seal on your own destruction."

He didn't know what she was talking about. It meant nothing to him that, for some unknown reason, she was opening the door of a wardrobe. The clothes and the shoes she hurled across the room to fall at his feet mystified him. The stick she took from the wardrobe after them puzzled him beyond measure. She held the thick, tapering ebony near the ferrule. "Those," she accused, glancing at the suit and the shoes on the carpet, "yours. This—yours." She thrust at him with the intricately carved, rounded ivory head of the stick, his father's stick, a family heirloom, known in Gunnarshaw. He gazed at the stains in the crevices of the carving. "It's enough," she said. "They're clever these days. Nobody's even attempted to clean it."

She savoured her triumph. He lived through a thousand lifetimes.

"These," she added. "And what else I can tell them. The blackmail you can't deny. The ruin that faced you if Gunnarshaw found out. The time I told Cluff you came in that night—"

"You can't know when she was killed!"

"The money in her handbag, the money you'd given her—"

"Who told you?"

She laughed again: "Your letter—"

"I never wrote to her."

"Wasn't it yours? Never mind."

He whispered, not to her but to himself, thinking of Jean on the road, a little while ago, his flight from Cluff and Barker, "There's no way out now."

"None," she said. "There never was."

"Tell them it isn't true."

"You ask that? From me? After our life together?"

## CHAPTER XII

THE TRUNKS OF THE PINE TREES SOARED BLACK INTO THE black night. The bulk of the house rose threatening. Cluff walked as if the gravel was eggs. Clive whimpered once, the whimper hardly audible.

"Stay, boy! Stay!" Cluff said, pointing to a spot under the trees.

He rounded the gable end of the house. The drive expanded into a wider area, flagged. He made no more noise on the flags than he had done on the gravel.

He listened. The wind soughed in the trees. Rain dripped from the branches. The wind and the rain silenced the more distant sounds of Gunnarshaw. Only a lessening of the dark over the roof, the reflection of its lights on low cloud, denoted the presence nearby of a town.

He groped for the handle of the kitchen door. He turned the handle and pushed. The door swung inward at his touch. The red eye of a dying fire winked at him from the grate. He looked at her legs, protruding from behind the table, regretting a little the time he had had to spend with Jean on the road, those other minutes he had wasted, purposely, in the drive after Barker in the car had disappeared down the hill on his way to Balaclava Street with Jean.

He knelt by the old woman. She wasn't dead. He thought Greensleeve, coming by the fields, couldn't have been much ahead of him.

He went into the passage, his ears cocked, making no sound.

He stood in the hall, looking about, through an open door into a dark room, at other doors closed, with no hint of light in the cracks between them and their frames.

The stairs turned back on themselves halfway up. He stepped on the inner edges of the treads, testing each one before he put his full weight on it to make sure it didn't creak and betray him. He stopped briefly at the head of the stairs, warned by a murmur of voices. He redoubled his caution, tiptoeing along the landing.

He had the knob in his grip. Words came to him in snatches. He released the knob and put his ear to the white-painted panel. He stayed where he was, listening.

Greensleeve sat on his wife's bed. She seemed to tower above him. She still had the stick in her hand. She pointed with the stick at the suit and the shoes.

She said, "I wore them."

His head drooped lower. His fingers scratched at the eiderdown. He didn't remember crossing from the door to the bed.

Her voice trembled with the intensity of the hate she had for him. "I followed you that night," she went on. "I've often followed you. I knew what you were going to do."

He said, "It was Carter I was afraid of when I saw her with him. I thought she must have told Carter what there was between her and me."

She demanded, "How long is it since we slept together? When have I been up at night waiting for you to come in? When did you ever come to my room before you went to yours?"

"You were out," he said, as if it had just occurred to him, "when I got back. I didn't know."

"I had to wait," she told him, "until I was sure you and the old woman were asleep. In the garden. It was cold."

"And Jean," he mused. "Not you," he said to his wife. "Never you."

"I was always the last one you thought of."

He asked quietly, "Did you kill her?"

She flung at him, "You killed her. It's all proved, up to the hilt. Even a man like Cluff must see it."

"Cluff made up his mind from the start."

"I saw you," she said, "going into the Town Hall. I saw her. I watched her in your car till you came. I saw you drive away with her."

"She made me go. She said Carter would marry her if I made it worth their while."

"I knew where you'd drop her," his wife said. "Which way she had to come to get back to Rupert Street. What else did you promise her to make her do that on such a night? How much more did she want so that you wouldn't have to risk being seen driving her through the centre of the town?"

He said, "It was something else every day."

"I saw the money," she said. "I hadn't time to read the letter. I heard somebody coming."

"Would you really have gone through with it?"

"In your clothes," she taunted him. "After she'd been with you in the car. With your stick."

"If it had been anyone else but you—"

"My word against yours. They'll never believe you, not when they know about you and her."

"You've been clever."

"It was you I wanted to get rid of."

He asked, "Where are you going?"

"To telephone."

"Don't!"

"You're a fool. It's either you or me."

"Please!"

"You're not poor. I deserve something in life after you're gone—"

She looked back at him, triumphant. He was on his feet. She opened her mouth and lifted the stick, suddenly afraid, regretting that she hadn't been able to resist gloating over him, that she couldn't have prevented herself from making it clear beyond doubt, while she could, who he had to thank for what would happen to him. She couldn't believe, he had been so crushed and broken, that he was reaching for her.

He grabbed at the stick. She fought for the stick and he tore it from her hand, simply, with an incredible, effortless strength. He lifted the stick to strike her.

She stared into his eyes. She began to scream.

Her screams mingled with the sound of a car engine in the drive outside. Barker, switching off the engine, heard the screams as he jumped out of the car. He glimpsed Cluff's dog, sitting on its haunches on the grass border, waiting for a word of release. He didn't stop to speak to the dog.

He didn't stop either in the kitchen, where the old woman was beginning to stir on the floor. He ran along the passage, up the stairs, on to the landing, tracking the screams to their origin, concerned for Cluff.

Cluff stood by the closed door of a bedroom. He had his hand on the knob of the door but he wasn't making any effort to open the door.

Barker said breathlessly, "Is it locked? Let me try to break it in."

Cluff looked round at him.

The screams ended abruptly.

Cluff shook himself. "I should have gone in," Cluff said.

"What—?" Barker started.

Cluff said, "I couldn't have told a tale like that in a court of law. She'd still have had him. There's Jean and the old woman. In any case, he'd have had nothing to live for once his affair with Jane Trundle came out."

He took his hand away from the door knob.

He added, "What other way was there? She'd never have admitted it. How could they have convicted her?" He said, "Who am I to interfere? The guilt was his just as much as hers."

"Sergeant," Barker pleaded, hurrying after Cluff.

"He won't run away again," Cluff said.

Barker heard the bedroom door opening. He looked back, past Greensleeve in the doorway, holding a stick, its head bloody, at Greensleeve's wife crumpled on the bed, her skull broken.

Cluff went down the stairs. Barker stood helplessly between the departing Cluff and the advancing Greensleeve. Greensleeve held the stick out. Greensleeve said, "You'll want it as evidence."

Barker took the stick. He stepped out of Greensleeve's way. "She's dead," Greensleeve said dispassionately. "It doesn't matter about Jane Trundle. They'll only try me once. This murder's the simplest."

Barker said, "Wait—"

"In the sitting-room," Greensleeve said. "I can't stay up here with her."

"Sergeant! Sergeant!" Barker was shouting again, torn between Greensleeve in a room off the hall, Cluff in the kitchen at the end of the passage.

Cluff was lifting the old woman. "You'll be all right," he was saying. "They'll send for a doctor." He put her in a chair.

"Sergeant!"

"There's a phone in the hall," Cluff replied. "Ring for Mole."

"If he escapes?"

"He's a chemist. It's up to him."

"But—"

Cluff shrugged: "I'll stay till they come then."

Uniformed constables followed Mole out of the police car. Cluff, in the drive, said, "In there. Barker's with him."

"You've done it again," Mole exclaimed. "How did you get on to it, Caleb?"

Cluff said, "His wife's upstairs. Look after the old woman."

He whistled to Clive. He set off along the drive. Someone was running after him. Barker called out, "The Inspector's in charge."

Cluff turned into the road, up the hill. He murmured, "I'll let Patterson know."

He didn't invite Barker to accompany him. Barker watched him in the light of the lamps in the road. Clive kept close to the Sergeant's heels. Barker could see the broad back and the shapeless trousers under the ancient Burberry, the heavy boots and the old tweed hat. The white patches on the dog's fur stood out in the night.

Barker stepped aside to let the car pass. The car stopped at the turn out of the drive. "I'm taking him to the station," the driver shouted, out of his window. Two men, a burly constable and Greensleeve, sat in the back.

The driver said, "Mole's still there. You'll be staying with the Sergeant until they get her away?"

Barker kept quiet.

The driver let the clutch in and moved forward. He added, before he was too far away for Barker to hear, "Where's the Sergeant got to, anyway?"

Also Available by the Same Author

# SERGEANT CLUFF STANDS FIRM

*'He could feel it in the blackness,
a difference in atmosphere,
a sense of evil, of things hidden.'*

Amy Snowden, in middle age, has long since settled into a lonely life in the Yorkshire town of Gunnarshaw, until—to her neighbours' surprise—she suddenly marries a much younger man. Months later, Amy is found dead—apparently by her own hand—and her husband, Wright, has disappeared.

Sergeant Caleb Cluff—silent, watchful, a man at home in the bleak moorland landscape of Gunnarshaw—must find the truth about the couple's unlikely marriage, and solve the riddle of Amy's death.

This novel, originally published in 1960, is the first in the series of Sergeant Cluff detective stories that were televised in the 1960s but have long been neglected. This new edition is published in the centenary year of the author's birth.

# MURDER OF A LADY

*Anthony Wynne*

Inspector Dundas and gifted amateur sleuth Eustace Hailey tackle a locked-room mystery in a Scottish castle.

# DEATH ON THE RIVIERA

*John Bude*

Counterfeit currency—and murder—darken the sunlit glamour of the Riviera. Detective Inspector Meredith needs to keep one step ahead.

# MURDER IN THE MUSEUM

*John Rowland*

The murder of an academic in the British Museum brings together Inspector Shelley and mild-mannered museum visitor Henry Fairhurst.

# THE SECRET OF HIGH ELDERSHAM

*Miles Burton*

When a pub landlord is stabbed, Detective-Inspector Young calls on "living encyclopedia" Desmond Merrion to help uncover the secrets of the village.